De

To Gill Foss

Best wishes +
lots of hugs!
Sherrill Wark

Refuge in l'Acadie

a Kesk8a story

www.crowecreations.ca

Refuge in l'Acadie

First Crowe Creations Print Publication June 2016

This is a work of fiction set against a backdrop of history.

Front cover photo © iStock, photo ID:24269934
Cover Design © 2016 Crowe Creations
Interior design by Crowe Creations
Text set in Garamond; headings in Clarity Gothic SF

Crowe Creations
ISBN: 987-1-927058-34-3

For Sue Pictou, yet another “cousin.”

Acknowledgements

Phyllis Bohonis, Evelyn Crete, Suzanne Keeptwo, Catina Noble, Sue Pictou, Marcel St-Amand, and Joe Wilmot, I can't thank you enough!

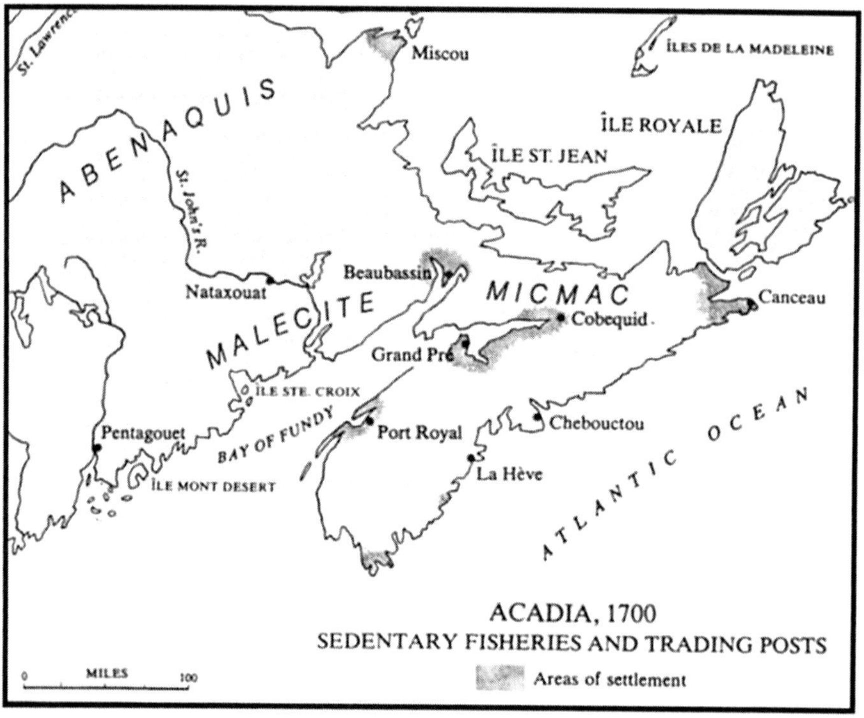
St. Lawrence
Miscou
ÎLES DE LA MADELEINE
ABENAQUIS
ÎLE ROYALE
ÎLE ST. JEAN
St. John's R.
Beaubassin
Nataxouat
MICMAC
Canceau
MALECITE
Cobequid
Grand Pré
ÎLE STE. CROIX
BAY OF FUNDY
Port Royal
Chebouctou
Pentagouet
La Hève
ÎLE MONT DESERT
ATLANTIC OCEAN
ACADIA, 1700
SEDENTARY FISHERIES AND TRADING POSTS
Areas of settlement
0 MILES 100

Foreword

The first in the planned six-book historical fiction series by Mi'qmaw storyteller, Keskoua, *Death in l'Acadie: a Kesk8a story*, has received excellent reviews and positive feedback and I can't say how delighted I am with this.

The editors and critiquers among my readership will be equally delighted to know that Keskoua, our narrator, is rapidly learning English and the [proper] use of the English pluperfect, subjunctive, future pluperfect continuous verb tenses (et cetera), and is expanding her English vocabulary in leaps and bounds, so is relying less on the Algonquian language's verb-based sentence structure. This excerpt about the Cree language (also an Algonquian dialect) from *Algonquian verb structure: Plains Cree* by Peter Bakker, Aarhus University, Denmark & RCLT, La Trobe University, Melbourne, Australia, might help explain things: "Cree is a typical polysynthetic language in the sense that almost all of the grammatical information is given in the verb, and very little in the noun. This means that verbs are frequent and also morphologically complex."

As of Book 2, *Refuge in l'Acadie: a Kesk8a story*, Keskoua is a mature young woman (28) with children and no longer the 15-winters-old, long-winded, dragger-out-of-sentences—and inserter of extra information between em dashes—that she was in Book 1. And you can trust me, a former editor myself, that the series is getting much easier to *write* because of this!

Even so, if you come across a section that seems to be particularly convoluted, imagine yourself sitting out by the Big Bear, sacred fire lighting up the faces of the dozens of people surrounding it, all waiting to be entertained by you, the Mi'gmaw storyteller, then read that passage out loud.

Poetic License

In 1694, when this book is set (and until 1697, this time), British forces controlled Port Royal. I chose to ignore this fact for the sake of story and to maintain character thread: all my French characters at the fort would have been shipped off to France!

Was Keskoua incorrect to say "the English fought with the French and often won?" Historically, yes; theoretically, no. In my research travels I learned, for example, that small groups of Dutch settlers from New England would stage raids and take over Port Royal for brief periods. Shall we call it "for a weekend"? The British would take over the fort for short periods as well. Warring was constant.

Also learned by researching obscure sources, meaning the losers' take on things: "History is written by the victors."—Walter Benjamin. Ah. No truer statement was ever writ.

SW
June 2016

It’s all about each other.

Near Port Royal, Acadia, Spring 1694

One

I was out harvesting cedar bark when my brother came running up to me, all out of breath. Some of our men had been out fishing, he said. A woman had floated up to them in a dugout. She told them the strangest stories. She'd had no water for three days, she said. When she told them she had come all the way from New England by sea in that dugout, they brought her to the village, thinking the woman had been drinking sea-water and had gone elue'wiet, crazy. So they sent my brother for me.

I grabbed my munti and tucked my tobacco offerings back into it along with my cedar bark and slung its strap over my neck.

"She's beautiful," Gi'gwesu said as we hurried along toward the village. "I wish I'd been the one to find her." Ahead and high in a tree, a group of titiesg, blue jays, were bobbing their heads up and down at a lone female. "She would think I'm a hero then, wouldn't she? Maybe fall in love with me?" The group of birds changed trees.

"Who found her?"

"One-Eyed Joe and Claude Guidry and Mathieu. They're old and have wives—well, not Mathieu." He smiled over at me. "Not yet anyways. So maybe I have a chance, e'e? Yes? She looks about twenty-three, twenty-four winters old so she's not *that* much older than me."

I stopped walking and turned to caress my brother's cheek as I tried to hide my smile. "Those men are not that far gone, my brother, but if anyone has a chance against them for her affections, you do. And if she is that beautiful, we'd better hurry before One-Eyed Joe takes her home and kicks his woman out of their wikuom."

This made my brother laugh out loud. "Do you think he would dare?"

A tities landed on the ground, crouched, then raised his head feathers. A racket above made me look up at two titiesg flying away. The female had made her choice. The other males were not pleased.

We began to walk again.

"Rabbit Woman has become strong, hasn't she?" There was nothing that could have made me happier than to see how my friend had changed over the last several years and that her husband, One-Eyed Joe, seemed to love her more every year.

"Do you think the Newcomer will like me?"

Gi'gwesu had seen twenty winters (eight winters fewer than me) so he was looking for a wife now although he wasn't looking very hard because he had many choices. He was not only handsome but he was a good hunter and a good singer and dancer, too. Many of the young women in our village looked up to him and I knew that Wasueg was hoping he would notice her over the others. He did, but he noticed the others, too. Almost as often.

"If this stranger is from New England like she claims," I said, "what happens to your heart if she is Puritan? They hate us. Even more than they hate the French."

"I know. I know. Oh, Keskoua, why must you always send reality into my life?" Gi'gwesu put his arm across my shoulders to hug me. "You storytellers are so careful about always telling the truth that it seeps in like the tide to drown all hope."

"You should be writing books like the ones Geneviève used to make me read when she was helping me learn how to write her language. Those books were sad. The men always died—mostly in battle—and the women went to convents. You sound just like them with your 'drowning all hope.'" A great squawking behind us told me that the remaining titiesg had found another female to impress. In the bird world, broken hearts heal quickly. We turned a corner in the path and a startled squirrel ran chattering up into the snawe'g, the sugar trees. "I don't want to see you get hurt. I don't want to see Wasueg get hurt, either. And stop exaggerating."

"Wasueg?"

I didn't have to look at my brother to know he was trying to put a look of surprise on his face. "Yes. Wasueg. Stop playing innocent. I know you like her. I know you spend time on the cedars with her."

"E'e. But I'm not ready yet."

When I saw the stranger, I knew why no man, after seeing her, would be "ready yet" to take a wife if he didn't already have one. Maybe even if he already did.

Two

By the time Gi'gwesu and I got to the village so had almost everyone else including Claude Guidry's wife with the youngest three of their eight children clinging to her skirt. I would not have wanted to be receiving the arrows that were shooting out of Marguerite Petitpas's eyes into my friend Claude's back. It was plain to see that Claude did not know she was behind him or he would not have been sitting on the ground so close to this beautiful Newcomer and leaning in. In the background, our Chief was guiding a very drunk Little Cock away from our Newcomer. Little Cock was waving his coin pouch in the air, the strings of his braided belt flying back and forth from it as he pleaded for her to go find his sister. As usual, anyone new was subjected to his crazy story about his sister being kidnapped by pirates. The surgeon from the fort was there too, and breathing hard, so he must have run the whole distance. Feather's husband was beside him, leaning over, hands on knees. He must have run to the fort to get the surgeon at the same time Gi'gwesu had come for me. Feather—or I should say Hélène as I had agreed finally to call her by her Baptismal name and not by her real name—greeted me from the other side of the clearing with a raised eyebrow and a glance at the woman and the gawping men who surrounded her. The baby girl on Hélène's hip leaned away from her toward me, smiling and stretching her arm out to make and unmake a fist to greet me. Jeanne, the daughter that had been put inside me without my consent when I was fifteen winters old, reached her hands out to stop Hélène's baby from falling. This made all three of them laugh because she didn't have to do that. Hélène had a good hold and the baby trusted her. Jeanne's laugh didn't stop when her eyes met mine. Claude and Marguerite had done the right thing when they told me they would raise her for me. She had become a confident, happy young woman coming up to thirteen winters. She'd had her First-Moontime Ceremony a summer ago.

Someone had rolled up a log for the woman and almost everyone else was either sitting cross-legged on the ground in front of her or crowded around beside and behind her. Not everyone from our village was there. One of the women had just finished having a baby. That's why I was away getting more cedar bark: we would be having a smudging ceremony to celebrate and I had almost none left. I saw that her husband, Second Son, was at their wikuom opening, staring over at everybody. I thought he would still be looking happy about having his first son, but his face was somewhere in the middle between angry and angrier. Second Son's moods changed really fast. That's what was dangerous about him sometimes. Years of drinking alcohol made it hard for him to change even though he wanted to and he went to the sweat lodge many, many times. Sometimes wanting and being able are two different ends of a gwitn, a canoe: no matter what end you're at you can see the other, but you can't be at both in the same moment. Two women were in front of their wikuoms, their break-fast fires still smoking, while their babies suckled at their breasts. One of them, whose husband was away hunting with his brother, was trying to keep her other little one from running over to see what was going on with the stranger.

The stranger's skin was dark but her features were like those of our people. Her hair was long and straight and black. Gi'gwesu was right, she looked to be about twenty-four winters old. Right now she looked much older than that, but I knew that when she was well again, she would be one of the most beautiful women I had ever seen. She was looking at her toes. Her feet were bare, her dress dark blue and hanging in strips and strings. Someone had given her a shawl to drape across her shoulders. It must have been Hélène as I knew the way she did her fringes.

When I looked around the crowd, I saw my husband leaning over to whisper something funny to his friend, Sleeping Cougar. Cougar saw me and poked Falcon in the chest with his elbow. Falcon's wider smile at me and his glance away told me that he and his friend had been discussing the Newcomer's physical qualities.

"I am Keskoua," I said in French as I approached the woman, lifting the strap of my munti from around my neck so I could reach inside it to bring out the moose hide ground-covering that I would set it on, about two paces from where she sat. "What is your name?"

"Silence," she said in English without looking up. Then in French, "*Silence*."

Several people sucked in air. Marguerite stepped forward, fists on hips, but before she could say anything, the woman spoke again. This time she said the word in our language: *Jenteg*.

Claude had straightened his body away from the woman the moment he caught sight of Marguerite's protruding belly from the side of his eye. The way his face went red made me want to laugh but I controlled myself. I was getting much better at holding in my laughter, and my thoughts, but I wasn't perfect yet (speaking of two ends of a gwitn). The seriousness of the situation made it easier. I stepped closer to the woman and Marguerite.

"Of all the impossible rudeness I have ever heard," Marguerite shouted at her, "this is beyond it."

"You speak our language," I said to the woman, sliding close to her like a lentug puts herself between her fawn and imminent danger.

"I do not speak it well," she said in English.

From beside her, Mathieu took the birch-bark drinking cup from her and replaced it with a fresh one. She tipped it up and drained the contents.

"How much water has she had?"

"One small container and now this," Claude said, rising from the ground and brushing off the seat of his pants. "We wanted to wait for you but…"

Marguerite's fierce eyes were now on his so he didn't finish his sentence but instead looked down at the Newcomer's toes then stepped back.

Mathieu continued for him. "She's been without for three days she says."

"Then we must forgive her rudeness." I threw my own arrows at Marguerite who shrugged.

I got a thank-you grin out of Claude from across Marguerite's shoulder.

Marguerite turned to the woman again, fists still on her hips, and asked: "So what *is* your name then?"

"Silence. Jenteg." She looked from her own toes to Marguerite's deerskin boots, up the long length of Marguerite's pregnant body to her face—Marguerite was almost as tall as I was—then over to my face. "You may call me Jenteg," she said "if you are more comfortable using your own language."

"That's your name?" my brother asked and I could tell that he had not one single thought in his head about laughing. "I've never heard of anything so strange. Jenteg. Silence. How strange."

I moved away to kneel down behind my munti and began to remove medicines and objects, the first my eagle feather.

The surgeon from the fort, Monsieur St-Amand, squatted beside me, arms across his knees. "What is your plan?" He spoke quietly. "If you want my opinion, I think she speaks the truth about coming from New England. She knows English. Did you hear that?"

"I did." I took more objects from my munti and laid them on the moose skin. "Look at her feet and ankles."

"And?"

"There's no swelling."

"Ah."

I stood up and returned to her. "Who said she was drinking seawater?" I expected to see Claude standing there ready to answer me, but he and Marguerite were walking away. By the set of their shoulders, his low and hers square and firm, I knew that if he had been a child, she would have his ear between her thumb and forefinger. "Anybody?"

One-Eyed Joe spoke up at the same time Mathieu did.

"She was talking crazy."

"Yes. Crazy."

"What did she say exactly?" Monsieur St-Amand asked, rising and closing the space between himself and the woman.

"That she came all the way here from across the Big Bay in a dugout," said Mathieu. "From Massawachusett."

"Great mountain place?" This was hard to believe. Maybe she *was* elue'wiet.

"She said she came by sea," said One-Eyed Joe. "I have heard stories…" He looked quickly at me. "Not from our people's storytellers, only stories from others…"

I bowed my head to him to say I understood his meaning. Our people's stories were handed down from storyteller to storyteller with nothing being changed. If it wasn't true, storytellers didn't say it.

Behind me, I heard the woman say a word I didn't understand and I turned my eyes around to see that Monsieur St-Amand was holding up a flat, round glass instrument and was looking closely at one of the woman's ears with it. She was leaning away from him slightly. Her eyes were like a frightened wolf cub's.

"C'est correct, c'est correct. Don't be alarmed," he whispered. "I am not going to hurt you."

I went back to my munti.

"I heard it was done before," One-Eyed Joe continued. "In a dugout it's possible. It's a strong craft against the sea." He looked down and moved his feet as if he didn't want to say the next thing he was going to say. "But a dugout is big. Heavy. And she… she's a tiny woman… And she would get weaker and weaker with no water."

Many people whispered "e'e, yes," then looked at Jenteg with respect.

Jenteg looked back down at her toes.

"So… all by herself… I don't know." One-Eyed Joe stepped back into the crowd of people surrounding us.

In English, Monsieur St-Amand asked her if she had been drinking seawater. She didn't answer him with words, she shook her head no.

"It's important," I said in my language. "The treatments are different." I had found what I needed in my munti: maple sugar sweets with a little bit of salt added.

She looked over at me again and I could tell that she did not like to have Monsieur St-Amand examining her the way he was. "I did not drink *any* water for three days. And I know what seawater does if you drink it. It makes you imagine things." She glanced over at One-Eyed Joe. "I didn't imagine my journey." She pushed Monsieur St-Amand's hand away when he moved around to peer into her right eye with his glass instrument. "Stop that."

Monsieur St-Amand moved away.

"And I was not alone for most of it."

My brother Gi'gwesu's face showed me the disappointment that was in his mind.

I gave her a sweet. "Eat this." I took the birch-bark drinking cup from her and gave it to Gi'gwesu. "Two of these half full right away. When Sun hits the top of that tree…" I pointed, "… two more, and also when Sun hits that one…" He was already starting off toward our water containers. "Come back here." I wrapped three sweets in a corn husk. "When Sun goes away, she gets one. Then water. When Moon is above our heads, another, then water. When Sun comes back, the last one, then water. After that, as much water as she wants. Understand?"

All I saw were the bottoms of his bare heels as he ran toward our water supply.

Gi'gwesu couldn't have been gone much longer than it takes a tities to hide an acorn, when J-B, one of Claude's sons, came running from the path his parents had disappeared into. He was ten winters old and already very tall so almost got his legs tangled when he stopped in front of me.

"Papa says to hide her." He pointed at the new arrival. "People are coming. For her. Three of them."

I glanced over at Jenteg and knew by the look on her face that she had heard J-B's words.

"They're bad."

Three

Monsieur St-Amand helped Jenteg to her feet as three of our men quickly stepped in. It looked like there would be more husbands getting their ears pinched that day—if not by their wives' fingers, by their wives' words. I didn't want to imagine how foolish our men and the Acadian men would get when this Newcomer recovered her health and her looks. Our people were welcoming and honest and trusting, but when a woman that beautiful made our man look away from us to her, it made us uncomfortable even though we tried to push that feeling away.

"You may come to our house," François told the woman. "We will hide you in our children's room." He paid no attention to Hélène's harsh look as she adjusted her baby on her hip then stepped in to slide the shawl with her free hand from the woman's shoulders up over her head. François was still a soldier inside, trained to protect the best way he knew how. I knew Hélène was used to this but it didn't mean she had to like it.

I turned back to J-B. "What did your papa say about these men? You said they're bad? How does he know that?"

"He called one of them Jacques. Jacques l'Itale, I think it was."

So Jacques l'Itale was not dead after all.

"And when Papa called him that, Mama's face took on a look I never saw on it before. She said to the man, 'No. You are dead. As you should be.'"

"We *all* thought he was dead, J-B. Tell me more."

"This man was translating for another who…" J-B's nose wrinkled like he was smelling something bad. "I didn't like him. I didn't like the way he looked at us. Like there was something like… I don't know. Something like anger but no feeling at the same time."

Over J-B's shoulder I could see that François and Hélène and the others had reached the edge of the clearing with the woman, Jenteg, invisible in their midst. I knew the word J-B was hunting for was "hate" but I was not going to put that word into his mind.

"What did your papa say?"

"He pretended to see something behind me in the bush and from the side of his mouth he said 'Go tell them to hide the Newcomer.'"

I knew then who these people must be. Hunters of men. "Ah, she must be a runaway slave." My thought came out of my mouth before I could shut it.

"What's a slave?"

I had to think about how to say it to this young boy. "It's a sad thing to be. It's like being with a chenoo, a wendigo, who eats you from the inside out."

"She is dangerous, then."

"She is not the chenoo. Those men are."

J-B's eyes went wide for a heartbeat then they closed to slits so I couldn't tell what he was thinking anymore. "I'll go see if Mama is all right."

"And I will go tell Hélène and François that the woman they are caring for is in great danger so that puts them in great danger, too."

J-B hesitated then turned back. "I hope those men don't find her. She looks nice."

It seemed that the beauty of our Newcomer was affecting everyone, even boys too young to go on their Spirit Quest time. "Tell your papa where she is hiding so he can keep those men away from there."

And away he ran.

Four

I could hear the loud voices of Hélène and François through the walls of their whitewashed wooden house even before I reached it. Gi'gwesu's face appeared at the window then went away. He opened the door. "I'm glad you're here. They are having trouble agreeing where to put her."

Jenteg was standing in the nearest corner, leaning against both sides of it, Hélène's shawl still over her head. Her eyes pointed down but I knew she was watching for any sudden movement toward her. Gi'gwesu went to her and slipped his arm over and around her like a robin protects her nestlings in a rain storm.

"If she is in the children's room, those men could harm them trying to get at her," Hélène told François as if he hadn't thought of this himself already.

"I can't protect her if she's out in the shed."

"So she is more important than our children now?" She put their baby girl into a basket near the doorway to the children's room. Two faces appeared at the edge of it, those of their sons, Georges and Ti-To, P'tit Thomas. Ti-To's eyes met mine but he didn't smile.

"Mon Dieu. You think I would jeopardize the children?"

"What did she do anyways?" Hélène threw this question at me with fish hooks on it.

"Put me under the floor," came a weak voice from behind me. "It won't be the first time."

We all turned—even Hélène's baby—to look at Jenteg.

"I'm not very big. I can fit in a small space. Lift those boards up." She pointed. "Get a *pá*. I'll dig the hole myself."

"A what?" asked Gi'gwesu.

"*Uma pá*. Une pelle."

"Ah," he said. "Something to dig with. Do you have anything, François?"

Gi'gwesu led Jenteg to me and pushed her against me. I had no choice but to put my arms around her so she would stay on her feet. The top of her head didn't quite reach my shoulder.

"You'll do no digging, Jenteg," Gi'gwesu said. "I'll do it." He was on his knees and curled over, tapping floor boards. "Which ones can we lift up?"

François was beside him right away and with Hélène's help, I got Jenteg to a chair on the far side of the room where she could rest against the table Claude had made for them. Together, he and Marguerite had stained and polished it and they gave it to François and Hélène as a wedding gift. There was no room—and no use—for an eating table like this (no matter how beautiful it was) in my family's wikuom, so Marguerite had made me and Falcon a wedding gift of blankets from sheep wool woven on her loom from New England. We still had them and used them.

Like a lentug, a deer, folding itself up on the ground to sleep, Jenteg slid a bent arm onto the table and laid her head down on it.

"Give her water," I said and both boys scrambled for the wooden water bucket on a small stand against the wall.

In their struggles over the cup, the bucket tipped over, spraying water everywhere. They stood there, chins low, eyes wide as they watched the water spread.

"Get the mop," said Hélène and Ti-To ran to the tall cupboard on the other side of the room.

Georges shrugged. "J'suis désolé, Mama. He bumped my arm."

"I'll bump more than your arm," said François without much intent as he pulled a screaming board out of the floor. "Get that cleaned up for Mama before it runs under here. Or wets the baby's basket."

"Oui, Papa." With cloths and the mop, the boys began to remove the water.

François turned to Gi'gwesu. "Don't stick yourself on those nails, Gig. You can use your knife to pry them out. Like this." He showed him.

Hélène grabbed four buckets out of a cupboard and said to me, "Let's get water. Together." Her eyes moved quickly to Jenteg on the chair then back to me. "We need to talk. Here, take these."

She almost threw two of the buckets at me.

"Georges?"

"Oui, Maman."

"When you boys are done with the floor, get the washing tub from the shed and bring it in here."

"Aww!"

"Do as your mother tells you," said François ripping a fourth board out of the floor. The hole was now large enough for Jenteg to crawl into but not large enough for Gi'gwesu to work in.

"Oui, Papa."

"And," added Hélène, "bring in wood to boost the fire. Our guest is getting a bath."

All four males turned first to Hélène then to Jenteg. Gi'gwesu's smile at the hopes of seeing our Newcomer without clothing was obvious. François turned his face away so I couldn't see his smile but I knew one was there. There were no smiles coming from the boys, they had a lot of work ahead of them and didn't like it. Hélène had taken on many of the ways of the Newcomers and especially of the Fathers. For *our* young ones, it didn't matter for most things whether they were girls or boys, they were all helping out as soon as they could walk. But the Fathers, the priests, taught that there were many differences between men and women, and their duties.

Hélène and I spent a good deal of time hauling water together while she spoke on and on about the difficulties involved in keeping our strange and beautiful Newcomer undiscovered by the slave hunters. "I will not have my children put in any kind of danger."

"I understand. I—"

"And I don't like the idea of her being around François at any time alone. He is a little too enamored of her. Don't you think?"

"I don't—"

"As it seems were all the men."

"Yes, it seemed but—"

"Cependant, however, we must help her just the same. It is our way."

"Yes. It is our way." I wasn't sure if it was still Hélène's way as she had become more and more French and Catholic than any of us. "The hole under the floor will be good in case they—"

"We will need to post a guard until those awful men leave."

"That's a good idea, Hél—"

"And we must keep Apalqaqamej from learning that this woman is in our midst."

I stopped walking and nearly dropped both my buckets of water.

"Apal! I forgot about her. Can we trust Second Son not to tell her?"

"It might best be left to One-Eyed Joe and some of our men to talk to him, e'e?"

I needed no reminding that Second Son always needed a threat to his life to do anything anybody wanted whether he wanted the same thing or not. I didn't like the idea of Second Son being harmed—especially the kind of harm he would need to be threatened with (he wasn't bad, he was just mixed up)—but sometimes we had to make difficult choices. Because of her childhood head injury, his wife, Apal, couldn't keep anything to herself. No secrets, no feelings, no words.

"I'll talk to One-Eyed Joe," I told her.

"What do you want to talk to me about?"

Hélène and I turned around so quickly, our buckets banged together, spilling water over the top of them onto the path.

With One-Eyed Joe were Claude and his son J-B, Mathieu and three men. One of these men I recognized even through his curly beard, medium-short hair and New England clothes. It was Jacques l'Itale.

"Hello, Jacques," I said. "We all thought you were dead."

"I am dead to all this." He opened his arms wide and looked at me along the length of his nose. "I am civilized now."

I don't know how I did it but I was able to keep words from spilling out.

"I heard you mention the name of Second Son's wife. Where is she?" Then he spoke quickly in English to the man standing behind him, a round man over fifty winters old with a cloud of meanness floating around him like fog. This was the man J-B had told me about. I got the feeling that the man was used to having people do what he wanted without daring to complain about it. A man like this would not have to threaten Second Son with anything; he would just have to tell him what he wanted.

Some of the words going back and forth between Jacques l'Itale and the mean man, I didn't understand. Even though the English fought with the French soldiers at the fort all the time and often won and took over the land for a while and tried to make us all speak English—even to each other—I didn't know anywhere as many words in English as I did in French.

These words from the mean man I understood: "Ask them if they've seen her."

Jacques l'Itale turned to me. "We're looking for a female. She has dark skin, long black hair and she is about this tall." He held his hand out, inside of it facing the ground, and at the level of his chin.

"Dark skin, you say." Hélène shook her head. "Does she have some kind of medical condition?"

"What do you want her for?" My mouth asked. "I mean… What would somebody like that be doing here?"

It felt like Jacques l'Itale was looking right into my eyes and could see what was hiding behind them. "You've seen her, haven't you?"

J-B moved around behind his father. I don't think Jacques or the mean man noticed this. The third man, short with arms that looked like they would split his shirt if he made the smallest move, was watching something up in one of the trees. Over one shoulder hung a musket, over the other a brown leather bag bulging with whatever was in it.

The mean man asked Jacques l'Itale: "What are these savages saying?"

"I think they know where she is, Maj—uh, *Benny*…"

Jacques l'Itale looked over at me to see if I had noticed this slip. I had but did not let my face show him.

"… however, I don't think you're going to get much out of them. We need to find the one named Apalqaqamej. She has something wrong with her head so can't keep anything in it. If she knows where the female is, she'll tell us. And happily."

"Excellent," said *Benny*. "Take me to her."

Claude whispered something and invisible as a snake in a corn patch, J-B slipped away.

Benny turned to the strong man. "Merit! Wake up. Let us give these savages some baubles."

The strong man came out of his dreaming about treetops to open his leather bag. He took out a handful of colored beads which he gave to Benny. I had been given so many of these things by the English invaders that I would never be able to use them all no matter how long I lived but we knew how to act when we were offered beads by Newcomers. Especially by dangerous Newcomers. Together as though in a rehearsed dance—which it was—Hélène and I put our water buckets on the grass and stepped forward, smiling like these were the first beads we had ever seen and talking to each other in our language—*how beautiful how rare how lovely how valuable mi'watm, I am thankful, mi'watm*—while Benny placed the beads on our opened hands two and three at a time.

Benny appeared to be pleased with his conquest.

We were.

Five

When she was still alive, people would tell the mother of One-Eyed Joe anything and everything about themselves because she was our healer. She would tell *me* their stories because I am a storyteller and was learning our stories to keep them in my head (and it turned out I was learning to be a healer, too, but didn't know it then). Many girls would tell Rabbit Woman things about themselves, as I had done when I was young, and she would sometimes tell me theirs, but only if it was important for me to know. When Geneviève was living in our village, she was another who was good at listening to the women, especially to the women with husbands who drank alcohol. There was nothing that could make her say "I never heard anything so terrible." She would also tell me what they had told her if she was worried about anybody. Geneviève was away now and nobody knew where exactly because nobody had seen her for many winters. I thought I saw her once, one morning back behind The Bear where her son used to go all the time but I didn't know if it was the memory of a dream I'd had about her or if it was real. I missed her. She was not one of our people but she was important to us and not just for listening. She had been teaching some of us to read and write French. Me especially.

I got most of the story of Little Cock from Little Cock himself. He took sick, really sick the evening after all our visitors showed up and he got worse as the days went by. It took six of us to get him up to the cabin at Mouse Ridge where he—and the rest of us, too—would be safe. It was almost another week before he came back from wherever the drink sickness had taken him, but once he got started talking, I learned a lot about him. Rabbit Woman was there, too, but he mostly talked to me about things—when his mind was working the way it was supposed to, I mean, and not making up its own stories.

Some of the things Little Cock told Rabbit Woman and me we weren't sure were real at first. We were both tending to him, sometimes taking turns sleeping outside in a wikuom while he went through the drink sickness. Ever since Paul Le Putois had tricked Falcon—before he was my husband—into going to the cabin at Mouse Creek to get him off the alcohol, we had used this place to cure our people from the drink sickness. This cabin made all of us feel sad because it was where, and partly why, Paul le Putois got shot. It was a good strong cabin with a wooden floor, a fireplace, two very small windows, the door could be locked from the outside, and it was far enough away from the village that people couldn't hear the screaming that sometimes came out of it. We had moved out the wooden cots and some of the other stuff a person could get hurt on if he started thrashing around too much. And it was better to keep only the things our people were used to instead of having Newcomers' objects like the heads of animals on the walls and clothing hanging on pegs that might turn into something different and strange when the drink visions came. So some of that stuff came out, too. We would change the kaksk'ug, the cedars, and the skins every time a new person came in. There had to be at least two people tending to someone coming off the drink because he could be dangerous to others, not just to himself. Sometimes, people didn't make it through the sickness so it wasn't something anybody should ever do alone. We all thought Second Son must have gone through a drink sickness by himself, maybe more than one time, because sometimes if an insect landed on him on a certain day in a certain way, he would run away screaming like it was a chenoo and not just a little bug. The whole village helped out in a way. People would come out to make sure everything was na to'q, all right, and that nothing had happened to those who were helping the one get through the drink sickness. Sometimes one of them would take over the watch for a while if we had other things to do. As a healer, I was needed elsewhere many times. We were extra worried about Little Cock. He had been drinking—as far as anybody could figure out—every day for more than twenty-six winters and through three wives. Nothing could have made him stop yet here he was, having what Monsieur St-Amand called *les saisies*, fits, just because Jacques l'Itale had returned to l'Acadie hunting for a beautiful slave woman from Massawachusett. I wasn't sure if Little Cock was ready to go back into his past to talk about what had happened to make him take up the drink for such a long time and then to suddenly stop it even though he knew it would make him terribly sick, maybe even kill him, but it was important for him to go back and remember then talk about it. It was part of the healing. He understood this.

He was pretty much finished with the visions and was able to keep down solid food when he began to tell us about what had happened to him when they took him away on the pirate ship. Sometimes he would start to say something then laugh so hard, we thought he would never be able to stop. The funniest thing about pirates, he said, was that even though most of them didn't believe in the Fathers or in what the Fathers said, pirates had ideas that were just as strange. One of the most different things was that every pirate treated every other pirate on his own ship the same.

"I didn't know that those from away could treat us like that. All the same. Just like we do." It didn't matter, he told us, what language you spoke or what color your skin was or what you might have done in your life, you were all equal. Except for Captain. Captain had power over everyone's life. "But still, we all shared equally in what we took from other ships according to how much work we did on the ship. Captain got the biggest share and even though I didn't know much at first, about the sea and sailing, I got a good share because I worked hard at the things I was able to do. And I learned fast."

I knew that Little Cock wasn't bragging.

"They were fair. Always fair. Honest with each other..."

This made me wonder why everybody said pirates were bad. The thing we all knew most about many of those from away was that they liked to feel superior and tell people around them what to do; then these people would want to feel superior so *they* would tell *other* people what to do; this went all the way down to the bottom guy who would then go home acting all superior over his woman and his family but not feeling it, so would get angry because he had all the superior on top of him and had to get rid of it somewhere. This was not our way, but some of our people were starting to do this anyway. Mostly when they got drinking alcohol. These are the stories I told you Geneviève heard about from women.

"Tell us more about the pirates." Rabbit Woman uncrossed her legs then re-crossed them to move the bottom one on top. "They sound like good people. We should hide them here when they are being hunted by the Spanish and the Portuguese."

"It's not always the Spanish and the Portuguese who do the hunting," Little Cock said before he squeezed his lips together and pushed his chin out. "It's everybody. There are some things I will not tell you about what we... about what the pirates did." With the back of both hands, he wiped off the moisture that had sprung from his eyes. "And probably still do to other pirates—and I mean the privateers to privateers and privateers to free pirates. I don't want to run those things through my head again because I want to think they weren't real." He turned his face away from us. "And I don't want to put nightmares in your heads either." He turned back. "The thing I will tell you is that on our own ship we were equal to each other, but if you were on another ship—especially an English one—you were mi'jan, excrement. Even worse if they caught you."

Rabbit Woman asked, "What's a privateer?"

Little Cock's lips curled like an alpha wolf's at a young male upstart. "Nobody anywhere liked us *free* pirates. They would hang us if they caught us because we didn't belong to anybody but ourselves. *We* were from *every* country—some of us from no country at all. The privateers were backed by their own Kings. If *they* got caught, their King brought them back to his country and gave them money and a good life. Nobody could hang them because they were 'soldiers,' their King would say. What those men did was acceptable because of the Rules of War, their King would say. We did the same or less but were condemned."

At first I thought Little Cock had decided to go off the drink because he, like every other man and boy it seemed, wanted to impress our beautiful Newcomer, Jenteg. But I soon learned it had everything to do with Jacques l'Itale, nothing else. But yet there *was* something else going on with Little Cock. I found out later that he had good reason to think it, but while Little Cock was going through his sickness back and forth, he kept saying that somebody had poisoned him. I didn't believe him at the time even though it wouldn't have surprised me if somebody had tried to poison him: he was always looking for a fight so made a lot of enemies. So when I thought about it back then, maybe somebody could have poisoned him. Maybe. A stronger maybe would be what had happened to him while he was on the pirate ship. Not to him exactly, but to his mind because of what they did to his sister Lilac. Lilac was twelve winters old when she disappeared. I was too young to remember anything about it, this is the part of the story that the mother of One-Eyed Joe told me. Little Cock had a bad reputation, yes, but he had been much kinder before they took him away. Everybody had liked him. He was the fourth child in a family of seven, and the only boy, so he took all his responsibilities extra seriously. He often said he would protect his sisters to his own death and this is what he thought life would be about for him. It didn't turn out that way.

Putting together what Little Cock and the mother of One-Eyed Joe always said, nobody saw the pirates come ashore that night and take Little Cock and his sister. They didn't even know pirates had been watching anybody. There were always many ships in the waters near the fort but the pirate ships usually didn't dare come in so close. They preferred the open sea because it was easier to escape from enemies there. It turned out that there was not only a pirate ship hiding near the fort, but an English one as well; and they were watching different people for different reasons. Nobody could have known where Little Cock and Lilac disappeared to. Nobody even had a dream to tell them that they had been taken together. Nobody thought, for sure, that they had been kidnapped by pirates. If they had thought about it, they would have asked the soldiers at the fort to get the sailors who came into the port there to look for them.

At first, everybody thought Lilac had gone away with a coureur de bois who'd been talking to her a lot, so they weren't worried about her so much. It happened all the time with our women, sometimes even the really young ones who were just curious to know what it was all about. People thought she would just show up again when she wanted to visit her family. Or when she tired of following a coureur de bois all over the place and having to do most of his work for him, and him getting all the money. By spring, though, they were wondering what had happened to her, and her family was especially getting worried. So One-Eyed Joe and his mother started asking people if they had seen her. The coureurs de bois sometimes lied to protect each other, but the mother of One-Eyed Joe knew, that this time, they were telling the truth. Their women hadn't seen Lilac either.

The man who had been seen talking to Lilac all those times—his name was Dupuy—told One-Eyed Joe and his mother that he and his woman had liked Lilac so would for sure tell everybody they met to ask around about her. He nudged his woman forward. The mother of One-Eyed Joe said that although the ancestors had often spoken of them, it was the first time she'd seen such a woman: tall and bony with yellow hair and pale blue eyes.

"Tell them, Gilla."

"My man here ask Lilac question from me." Gilla's pale eyes held great concern in them. "My words is not good. Not know… Not know…"

"She's trying to say she doesn't know your language. She liked that young girl's beading work on her… her… What do you call them things? Comment dit-tu chaussons? Ah, oui. Moccasins! Moccasins. The beading on her moccasins." The man put his arm around Gilla. "I learned how to do beading from that girl. That Lilac girl. Can you imagine?" His laugh wasn't a strong one but it was kind. "Me doing beading?"

"*Beee-ding*," said Gilla nodding her head and smiling wide. "*Beee-ding.*" She held out one moccasined foot for them to see. The beading had been well done, the mother of One-Eyed Joe said. When Gilla put that foot back on the ground, she curled the other one around behind it but not before they noticed the clumsy beading on it, her practice moccasin. (It seemed there had been many Bennys handing out beads to more than our people. And equally as un-generously as Benny would dole them out to me and Hélène years later.)

The mother of One-Eyed Joe was then satisfied that Lilac had not run into trouble having one of the coureurs de bois take her away; and none of our hunters had found any sign that she had been hurt by an animal and died in the bush, either, so they accepted that she was just gone somewhere. People still told the story around the fire for years after that, trying to make themselves believe that she and Geneviève were wandering around through unknown places together even though we knew in our hearts they weren't. It was a way to stop worrying about her by a little bit.

About Little Cock, though, everybody worried right away. He was a message runner and was important not only to the people in our village but in the villages around and most especially, he was important to the French soldiers at the fort. He was able to run through the bush—no matter how thick with trees and vines it was—like a snipe. He could do this ever since he was ten winters old, so this is where he got his name from. He could run from our village to the next one and back again with an answering message in less than half a day. Even after he returned from being on the pirate ship, he could still run as fast after he got what he called his "land legs" back. We used to say that if he had a wind behind him, he could get to the next village before a Snowsnake spear could get there. Drunk or not.

He was just under fifteen winters old when the pirates kidnapped him and took him away on the pirate ship. We knew this happened a lot but it hadn't happened to any of the people in our village. The pirates would sometimes keep the men they kidnapped, but then they wouldn't be kidnapped anymore, just part of the crew and usually happy about it. More often, they would sell them as what was called "Indentured Servants" to the people in New England. It wasn't just those with dark skins who paid for their keep this way, even the coureurs de bois in the Settlement at Québec did this when they came from the land of Claude's King; and so did the men who worked for the Hudson's Bay Company and came from the land of the Maudits anglais. Claude explained it to me one time. He said he would never be anyone's servant no matter what. He said that seven days in the bush was a long enough time, so seven years working for somebody else and getting nothing in return was seven eternities and he'd rather spend sept éternités in Hell than work for les Maudits anglais in

Hudson's Bay and would rather spend *fourteen* eternities in Hell than work for the Puritans in New England.

One-Eyed Joe always said this indentured servant idea was why nobody thought that pirates had taken Little Cock for that. Why would anybody want to buy a skinny Mi'gmaw boy who was good only for running? But Joe's words made the people think further: Maybe the English had taken him away because he was important to the French at the fort? That was possible. The last thing anybody thought of was pirates.

Nobody knew anything for sure (and not even then, really) until Little Cock came back stumbling drunk into our village one afternoon about three winters after he and Lilac had disappeared. He was throwing gold coins around like a squirrel tossing pine cones down on your head when you got too close to her nest. He had brought a huge locked iron trunk along with him. By the time the sun went away that day, what would eventually become Little Cock's own personal chenoo showed up in the form of Jacques l'Itale. This was a mystery I found really difficult to understand, that this man, this Jacques l'Itale, would keep following Little Cock around like he was a little child tied to his mother with a long cedar rope while she picked berries. It was not a rope woven out of love, but a rope woven out of something I will never understand and hope I never experience.

It had been sailors from an English ship who had captured Little Cock. At least, the English sailors had *tried* to capture him. He told Rabbit Woman and me that something had gone wrong, though, and the men off a free pirate ship had jumped in to save him.

None of this made any sense to anybody because all Little Cock would say for the twenty-three winters since he came back to our village (and I heard it many times over, too), was:

"I hate the man for what he did to my sister, but at the same time I am grateful to him for saving my life. He ruined my sister. Then he saved her.

Then he ruined her even more. Please go to The Colonies for me and find her. Here. I have coins. They're gold. Real gold." And he would place coins into people's hands like Newcomers put beads into them, even holding their wrists and folding their fingers over on top of them. "Witches took her. Witches. Please. Go find her for me. I have to get her back. Please help me. No. I can't go. I must stay here. If they catch me, they'll hang me. How can I look after my sisters if that happens? How can I save them from that man?"

Nobody believed that pirates had taken him and Lilac. Nobody believed him about *witches. Witches* took his sister? They didn't think he even knew what witches were. (*They* didn't.) And especially after Jacques l'Itale showed up later the very day that Little Cock returned. Jacques l'Itale being "that man" but denying it, mouth opened wide, head back like a singing wolf, and howling, but with laughter. If nobody believed Little Cock before, they certainly didn't after Jacques l'Itale told them nothing was true. It was the drink made Little Cock have visions, Jacques l'Itale told the people. It was pure imagination from the drink saying that Jacques l'Itale had been the one to kidnap Little Cock's sister. "Kidnap a child? Ridiculous!" *Assolutamente ridicolo* that he would lose her then follow Little Cock home to our village! Why would he do that? "*Io non sono stupido.* I'm not stupid."

Jacques l'Itale continued to deny everything and there was no reason not to believe him because he was kind to our people and thoughtful even though he drank alcohol just as much and as often as Little Cock did. Pretty much everybody liked Jacques l'Itale and believed everything he said. That is, until Jacques l'Itale began to take up with Little Cock's younger sisters as predicted by Little Cock. The people believed less that came out of the mouth of Jacques l'Itale and a little more of what came out of Little Cock's mouth after that.

Then later on, when Jacques l'Itale took up with Little Cock's eldest daughter before her first Moontime, the people turned against Jacques l'Itale and begin to think that maybe there was something to Little Cock's story after all; perhaps some truth to why there had been so many fights between the two men over the years, each accusing the other of being a liar and ruining lives; with Jacques l'Itale, right to the end, swearing on his mother's life that he had never laid eyes on Little Cock until he arrived in our village; that he knew nothing of this supposed sister; that he most certainly had done nothing to Little Cock's daughter that she hadn't wanted, asked for, demanded; that Little Cock was nothing but *un bugiardo*, un menteur, a liar. Jacques l'Itale had never even *heard* of our people until he washed up on shore at the fort. And no, he had come off an *Italian* ship, not that pirate ship somebody had spotted in the cove with its Captain hanging from the yardarm upside-down and dead. How could anyone be so *stupido* as to think otherwise. This reminded me of how they said Claude Guidry had landed up in our village. But Claude had come by land through the bush and this was where he got his name La Verdure, The Woodsman, and we believed him. Jacques l'Itale's name should have been Talking Out Of Both Sides Of His Mouth.

The fights after Jacques l'Itale had taken up with Little Cock's daughter became much more serious so we couldn't understand why Jacques l'Itale didn't just go away or why Little Cock didn't just outright kill Jacques l'Itale. Then, the last anybody saw of Jacques l'Itale was the day after Paul le Putois died.

Our first thought was that Little Cock had finally killed him somehow. It would have been a good time to try when everybody was so distracted with the slow, agonizing death of Paul le Putois. The soldiers had captured La Grossesse, the man who had gut-shot Paul le Putois out of an old revenge. The soldiers had taken Little Cock away with them, too, but had let him go the next morning because he was shaking from the lack of alcohol and there was no one at the fort who wanted to deal with it. They just gave him a bottle of rum and set him free. I heard later that Little Cock had tried to poison Jacques l'Itale, that he had put something in the rum then offered it in the way of a truce, but I never believed it. But when Little Cock kept saying, while he was going through the drink sickness just after Jacques l'Itale had showed up again, that somebody had poisoned *him*, it made me wonder. I said nothing. I kept this to myself.

Over the years, Little Cock had continued to offer gold to those passing through our village and to any new soldiers at the fort, whether they were the English ones or the French ones. At gatherings, he would walk around to those from other villages, offering them gold. But nobody agreed to help him no matter how many gold coins he pressed into their palms. What did we need with gold? And the soldiers—whether they were the English or the French ones—thought he was a crazy man setting them up to take bribes which would only have them end up standing at the wrong side of a firing squad.

We believed little until after the drink sickness overtook him, did what it wanted with him, left him exhausted, hungry and cold, and wanting—needing!—to talk. Rabbit Woman and I were with him outside the cabin at Mouse Ridge in the fresh air that afternoon, sitting on the ground around the fire pit, he with extra skins under him and around his shoulders because he was skinny from the years of neglect so always cold. The bush, not quite fully wakened from an extra cold winter, was quiet around us. It was ready to listen, too. Little Cock started talking.

***

"Captain was furious when he learned that not only had some of his men debarked against his orders but that they had debarked to bring a woman back on board with them. On top of that, they had deceived him by hiding her away in storage. And he didn't learn about this woman until they were well away from land and almost at the coast of Massachusetts—two weeks later. He was so angry, he threatened to throw everyone on board over the rail. He wasn't awfully angry about me when he found out that I had lied to him about everything. He said he would lie to protect his sister, too. '*BUT WOMEN ARE NOT ALLOWED ON SHIPS*,' he informed me with his nose right up to mine. 'Women bring storms.'"

"I know they can *cause* storms in the home of Claude Guidry and Marguerite Petitpas," I joked.

Rabbit Woman covered her mouth with her hand but she couldn't keep the laugh from coming out of her eyes.

"Captain ordered the one who had taken Lilac to throw her into the sea."

I stopped laughing. Rabbit Woman gasped.

"The man begged Captain to allow him to wait until the next port. They were closest to Boston. It would only be another week or so—if the good sailing weather held up. He would put her ashore there, he said. He would take her in himself. He knew people in Boston who would take her in, who would be kind to her, treat her as one of their own. I opened my mouth to tell Captain that I'd go too, but one of the others told me I'd best keep silent or I'd be the first to go over the rail. I was still new. They didn't know me or trust me yet. Especially after learning I'd lied about her presence not only to Captain but also to all of them, except for this one's booty fellows who already knew about her and where the man had hidden her.

"The other men grumbled and complained about this man's stubborn insistence. Many of them wanted her overboard. They were afraid.

"The man who took Lilac claimed to be Italian. Someone told me later that he was no more Italian than I was. That he was Portuguese. Maybe even Spanish. He was loud and passionate though, so could have been any of these. He most certainly wasn't English. From what I've learned and seen, they're all words and nose in the air and he wasn't like that. He said he would agree to having her naked as long as the other men promised on their mothers' graves to leave her alone."

"Naked?" Rabbit Woman and I said together.

"Naked women send storms away."

I couldn't help myself. I laughed. But the sadness coming from Little Cock's eyes made me stop right away. "I'm sorry."

"She was hardly a woman. Still a child. One of the other men, I can't recall his name—his face was terribly scarred on one side and down his neck—made note of this and said, 'We should toss this self-named Italian into the sea instead. This bastard, not the girl.' I didn't trust what any of them might do, but there was nothing I could do unless the entire crew was on my side. Nowhere I could go. No way I could escape from that ship with Lilac and save her."

Rabbit Woman's hand reached out to touch Little Cock's knee. "I'm sorry. So very sorry."

"I must tell you something. This 'Italian' man called himself Giacomo. In French, it's Jacques." Little Cock's eyes said much more than the name.

Rabbit Woman and I looked at each other. "Jacques l'Itale?" she whispered. "That's where he came from?" And Little Cock made us promise never to repeat that name in his presence ever again. "So it's true then. Everything you ever said was true and everything he ever said was a lie."

"I also heard him once called Jacobo, said the Spanish way. A man on ship called him that once and the bâtard turned his head right away to the name then back again when he caught himself. The man who called him that name laughed and said 'I thought so, you lying dirt.' By morning, that man was no longer anywhere to be found. He'd gone over."

"… It really *was* him who took your sister so many years ago…" Rabbit Woman seemed to be away somewhere else.

I said: "He really truly *was* lying all along. I'm sorry, Little Cock. And I'm also surprised you didn't kill him many times over."

"It wasn't that I didn't want to." Little Cock breathed in so deep and so long I thought I felt the trees around us bend inward. He let it all out and his breath took just as long to go out as it had to go in. Something small skittered through the undergrowth behind him. "I couldn't. He knew that. That's why he taunted me. He knew where Lilac went when he… when they… He laughed and said it was witches, but now I wonder if that was true or not."

"Na to'q, na to'q."

"As long as he was alive, I had a chance to find her again. I thought maybe, by some luck or chance, he might some day tell me. Perhaps if I got him drunk enough." He looked over at me with his half-smile. I didn't return it. "But when he took up with yet another of my daughters, my youngest girl—it seemed he was finished with her older sister—I'd had enough. I knew Lilac would understand my need to protect my own child from this… this monster. I felt inside that Lilac had gone on her Journey many years ago. I made my decision to do it when they had me locked up the day of that… the day of that mess with the boy with the big eyes. I can never remember his name."

He meant Paul le Putois but I didn't move or say anything. Little Cock needed to get this out of himself.

Something else made a noise back in the trees, perhaps the potential mate of the first creature. Once again, it was something small and it wasn't running from fright. Yes, life goes on in spite of everything that affects the rest of us.

"I didn't want to use a musket. It would make a noise. If I used a knife, *he* might make a noise." Little Cock hung his head. "Such a coward I was. I didn't want anyone to know it was me. I didn't want to hang for this mi'jan. How could I find my sister if he was dead? So I had to think of something. I wanted to be certain…" The laugh coming out of Little Cock was uncontrollable and lasted until he began to cough. He sipped water from the birch bark cup beside his knee. "I wanted to be certain he didn't make any noise while I was close to him when he died." Little Cock spat on the ground. "The poison I gave him didn't kill him, it only made him sick. But at least it scared the bâtard enough to make him finally go away." Little Cock made eye contact with me, then with Rabbit Woman. "By your faces, I see you aren't judging me for that?"

We shook our heads.

"Why did he follow you here?"

"I saw him kill Captain. I was the only one to see it." Little Cock shrugged. "This was the real reason I left the ship. It was not that I escaped my captivity. I was not a captive. I was enjoying my life. Most of it, anyway. I was enjoying the gold and the power it bought me at various ports. It gave me security. No. I didn't escape my life on that ship. What I escaped was certain death at the hands of that murdering bâtard, Jacques l'Itale."

"He followed you to kill you," said Rabbit Woman.

"No one kills a Captain without sentencing himself to being hunted for the rest of his life. Neither free pirate nor privateer will allow a Captain-killer on board his ship. They'll kill him themselves if they find him."

"But he didn't kill you," I said. "Why not?"

"I don't know for certain." Little Cock stood up and shook his legs one at a time. "How long was I in that… that other world? I can't remember being so stiff and sore." He sat down cross-legged again.

"Longer than some and not as long as others," I said to comfort him. "We have to put some things behind us."

"I don't remember a lot. It… It frightens me to know that drink made me forget things and not drinking made me forget things, too. When will I remember?" He turned to the trees as if hearing a sound but there was no sound this time. "When will I remember the terrible things I did to people?"

"Right now it's important to think of the *good* things you did to people."

He laughed.

"Na t'oq?"

He nodded.

"So why didn't he kill you? What stopped him? There must have been a big reason."

"I have two ideas. One is that he couldn't kill me without everybody knowing he was a killer. If he killed me, people would realize it was to keep my mouth shut about Captain. Everybody had seen Captain hanging from the yardarm and heard who the crew blamed for killing him. Me or l'Itale. If I killed l'Itale, they'd think it was me killing the witness. If he killed me? They'd know it was him who killed Captain." Little Cock laughed. "We couldn't kill each other without getting ourselves hanged for something else. Plus all that, he needed somewhere to hide."

Rabbit Woman stirred the fire and a few sparks rose into the air like daytime stars. "Do you need more water?" she asked him.

He shook his head. "The other idea is something I learned from being on the pirate ship and learning about people and the world. There's a certain kind of man who cannot tolerate anything bad in himself so he takes it away from inside him and puts it into somebody else. He believes then that he never did this thing he did. There is never anything in his face or actions that will give away his lie because there is no lie in him. To him, he didn't do anything. The other person did."

I crossed my arms. "To think everyone believed him and not you all these years."

"In his mind," Little Cock said, "he thought he had done a good thing for me. Killing the man who had put my sister ashore. He thought himself a hero. Couldn't understand why I hated him so much. He was the one who did that to my sister. He. No other."

"Did the crew come looking for him? They knew he was the one who did it, didn't they?"

"We both left the ship around the same time, remember? They assumed, wrongly of course, that I must have been a party to the killing, too. Not just l'Itale. The connection was Lilac. When some of the crew came ashore, they said they were looking for an Italian and a little short Indian called L.C. That was me."

"But the soldiers did nothing."

"It was still mostly the same group of soldiers who were here when I disappeared. Their three-year term was just coming to an end so they all remembered me. Everybody was always still watching for me and Lilac, not just those from our village and the villages around. The soldiers were happy I'd come back." Little Cock smiled on one side of his mouth and the corners of his eyes wrinkled. "They missed me. They missed me as a runner. But it wasn't just that they were happy to have their runner back and were prepared to protect me, they didn't want to get involved with the death of a pirate Captain. And pirates were a nuisance for them, too. Especially free ones. I think they weren't very concerned that a pirate captain was dead. Why would they care who might have done it? They sent the crew away and threatened to sink their ship if they weren't gone by the next tide."

"Did they go?"

"They did." He held out his drinking vessel. "I'll have some more water after all, Rabbit Woman. Thank you."

Rabbit Woman took the cup and went behind the cabin to fill it from one of the water barrels there.

Little Cock leaned toward me. "The soldiers knew where that bâtard l'Itale was hiding. They thought we were friends." He spat on the ground. "That we had done it together. One of them told l'Itale where to find me.

And there he was. All happy and pleased with himself for doing me this… this *favor*." Little Cock lowered his head and shook it. "Favor? Killing one of the few men who knew where Lilac went?"

Rabbit Woman came back with the water and handed it to him.

"And that's not all. That's not the worst about this man." Little Cock took a sip of water and shivered. He set the cup down and pulled his rabbit skin blanket higher up on his shoulders. "He was hoping to replace Lilac."

"What?"

"When he first grabbed her, I remember she said, 'No, don't take me. I have a family that needs me. Many sisters who need me.' Yes. That's where he must have learned about the others. Because of what followed, I had forgotten. But wait… I just realized something… She said it in our language and he understood. How many languages does this man understand and speak? Who is he? Who is he really?"

All three of us turned our bodies and eyes around to search the snawe'g and kaksk'ug behind us. There were no sounds coming from the bush. It was like every tree, every rock and every small creature was listening. It made me, for one, wonder what they all were listening for. Little Cock's words? Or something else?

"He adopted almost all of our ways and this made our people accept him even more. He hunted and fished with our people. He was friendly and liked by everyone. We began to wonder if he might be one of those who loves men. Two of my older sisters were of the age to be taking a husband but he wasn't interested in them, only in the younger ones. But they would not go with him. At least *they* believed me." He let a short laugh come out of him. "I think they did, anyway. Maybe they just knew.

"Back when he took Lilac, the bâtard had been watching her for over a week. Desired her. These pirate ships can anchor off almost any coast without being seen if her sails are down." He looked at us and laughed. "Or have their Captain hanging from the yardarm, e'e? It's always amazing how invisible trouble gets when nobody wants to get involved with it."

This made me smile, not because it was funny, but because he was making jokes. It meant Little Cock was starting to feel better about himself.

"Whenever the crew of their ship needed to stock up on supplies, a small party would first go ashore to steal clothing. Wearing these stolen clothes, three or four men would put a boat in the water and pretend they were fishing. Sometimes they would do just that while they drifted—*hah*, drifted by means of a cleverly played oar, that is—closer and closer to where they really wanted to be. In full view, and nobody ever notices or cares. Do you remember when this hap—? No. You women wouldn't. It was too long ago. At the fort, for maybe a week or so, they were suddenly missing supplies and equipment. Sometimes musket powder but most of the time salt, flour, hams, lard, biscuits, beans. Even chickens. I don't know how they kept those noisy things quiet. And two suckling piglets from their sow one day."

This made me think of Gesm'pisit, one of Claude's mama pigs from my younger times, one of the ones I had named and had made Claude promise never to let get cut up for sausage. Hearing that these men took a piglet—two of them—before it was time for it to leave its mama made me both sad and angry.

"The men at the fort blamed our people of course, for taking these things. Can you imagine? We had no need to steal food. Especially their food the way they prepare it. It makes our people sick. We didn't steal anything."

Rabbit Woman and I muttered agreement. "It's not our way."

"Except from the tavern." Little Cock closed one eye at me and tried to stop the smile that jumped onto his face but he couldn't. The smile went away quickly. "I can't believe the foolish things I did because of… Because I was foolish to start with, e'e?"

"E'e. But you were going through a bad time."

"I was. Yes. But that was no reason to— *AH!* I don't want to start feeling sorry for myself. That's what started it all. If you go too far inside yourself, especially if you have a big enough reason, no one but you exists anymore. No one else on earth matters but you."

Rabbit Woman reached out again to pat his knee.

"Let me continue before I get going somewhere else. Or before I have another… What do you call it?"

"Fit. Are you not feeling good? All is na to'q?"

"Yes. All is na to'q. Thank you. L'Itale was one of the men assigned to the work of replenishing the ship's supplies. Pirates rarely purchase anything they can take for free. Why not?" Little Cock raised his eyebrows, tipped his head to one side and raised his shoulders and his hands, palms up. "He was in charge of the shore party. I don't know when it happened, but he caught sight of Lilac on one of the first trips ashore. She was in a clearing talking to some people and laughing. This is what one of the men told me anyway. Who knows if it was true? Makes sense though, because from that time on, he sent the party ahead to take supplies from the fort while he stood guard—so he called it—but instead, he hid in the bushes so he could watch her some more.

"When Captain was satisfied with the amount of stores brought on board, l'Itale asked for one more trip, suggesting three of his close booty fellows go with him. None of the original party. Captain refused, but they went anyway. That's why Captain was so angry. You don't ever disobey Captain. But when they came back on board… And this was at night, without Captain's awareness… They hid Lilac in a storage room after telling her they'd kill me—they brought me too—if she let anyone be aware of her presence. They told me they'd kill *her* if I said anything. To distract Captain and to appease his anger, they brought a small cannon back with them and left it right in the middle of the deck, with me tied to it. I don't know where they got it. I think from another ship. These men were good. Captain would see this first thing on awakening. We were already at sea when Captain came out of his cabin.

"I heard one of the crew bid him good morning and when I turned, I saw a combination of joy and rage on his face when he saw the cannon and me. Captain was pleased about the cannon and this is why he didn't throw them over the rail for disobeying him. They got three lashes each for doing it, but at least he didn't kill them. You never disobey Captain's orders. It turned out that he was also pleased about me. Eventually." Little Cock shivered and moved closer to the fire.

Rabbit Woman put another piece of wood on it.

"Lashes?" I asked. "He gave them eyelashes? A gift of eyelashes?"

"Nothing as kind as a brush of eyelashes on their backs, Keskoua." Fist closed around an imaginary object, he made a long swinging motion of his arm to show he was striking something with the object. "Lashes by a cat."

"A gajuewj?" asked Rabbit Woman, her laugh trapped in her mouth by her hand again.

"Not that either. A whip." He held up his hands close together, tucked in one thumb, and wiggled everything else. "With nine strings of unraveled rope, knotted near their ends. They told me the one made of leather hurts even more."

"Captain was a cruel man," I said.

"Kind enough to let it be rope. Kind enough not to toss them over the rail. And kind enough to save my sister's life later. He did not know about her yet. If he had at that time, when his rage was at its height, there would have been six of us feeding the fishes. He asked about my bruises." Little Cock touched one cheek, an opposite shoulder, the knee on that side.

"For the safety of my sister, I couldn't tell him the truth so I just told him that I had fallen on the way. And yes, that I had come voluntarily. I had to lie to him, but I will tell *you* the truth. I swear it will be the truth. It always was the truth."

"We know only part of it," said Rabbit Woman. "I, for one, never heard you say more than accuse Jacques—I mean, that bad man, sorry, I'm not supposed to say his name—of taking your sister away. I didn't believe you. Nobody did. So please. Tell us what really happened."

"I first saw one of l'Itale's booty fellows behind a tree. Just the edge of his hat and part of his eye. He was watching my sister in the clearing as she sat there alone, braiding cedar bark. From the intensity on even only that part of this man's face, I knew he was planning to take her. I saw no others. As I came out into the clearing to warn her and stand ready to fight this man, I was jumped on by three English I had not seen. They had been hiding in the trees behind. Watching *me*. This is when l'Itale himself and his three booty fellows jumped out and caught my sister before she could even realize that something was going on. I was fighting English men and my sister was fighting men I did not know. Men who were dressed like Acadian men but I didn't know any of them so knew the stories I'd heard about pirates sometimes disguising themselves in stolen clothing must be true. Pirates. Taking my sister. I could think of nothing worse. I fought the English men as hard as I could but they were too strong and there were three. The first thing they did was take my knives out from my belt and my ankle straps and toss them away. I am so ashamed."

"You were… what? Fourteen winters old? Strong, but not as strong as three grown men together."

"I know what you're saying, Keskoua, and you are kind to say it. I was small, too. I still am. They began to drag me backwards away into the trees but Lilac put up such a fuss that one of the men—it was l'Itale himself—took pity and told his men to help me get away. 'I can take care of this little female on my own,' l'Itale told his men, with her kicking and trying to scream behind his hand.

"These English had no muskets with them, or other defense that I could see, so when l'Itale's three fellows came at them waving knives, the English men dropped me and fled. I dusted myself off and as I turned to thank the fellows I saw that l'Itale was now holding a knife to my sister's throat. He said, 'Lest you betray us, it is best you come with us. Or she'll die.'"

"Jacques l'Itale saved you from the English. He saved your life."

"Maudit bâtard," he said. "Mine, yes. And when Captain discovered her on board, l'Itale saved my sister's life, too. Her physical life. But not her spirit from what I heard happens when— when women are put ashore in one of those ports. When there is no one to protect them." Little Cock hung his head down. "If only I'd been bigger. Stronger."

"You can't change how tall you are just by wishing. I know *that* for sure."

Little Cock smiled at me but only with his mouth. "After Captain found Lilac in the storage room, spent his rage on l'Itale and the others and had calmed down, he learned her age. When he learned that she was young, barely a woman yet, he went into another rage. It was then he agreed that l'Itale could put her ashore. But l'Itale would have to sell her and divide the money among the crew."

"Or ...?" I asked.

"I told you, there was never an *or* when Captain gave orders."

"How did Captain find her down in the storage room?" Rabbit Woman asked him. "I thought these Captains and Lieutenants and men like that never have to do any work. That people always did things for them. Why would he go to the storage room?"

"He didn't need to this night. L'Itale would visit her in the evenings down there."

"And?"

"One evening she cried out."

"She cried out for help? Was she no longer afraid of putting you in danger?"

Little Cock shook his head and put his head down again. "If only I…"

I spoke. "What did you say about not taking that trail of feeling sorry?"

"Oh. Wait. I understand," said Rabbit Woman, biting her lip. "He forced her to—"

Little Cock nodded, raised his head and adjusted the rabbit skin blanket on his shoulders again. "Captain had finally made his decision and with good wind and good weather we soon arrived close enough to the port at Boston to be able to go ashore. Captain sent l'Itale and two men who loathed him so would ensure he returned to the ship with the money—the one with the scarred face was one—to take her and sell her. The party didn't return until almost dawn."

Rabbit Woman leaned forward and whispered, "Captain didn't let you go, too? To make sure she was going to be na to'q? That they didn't sell her to anyone that might cause… might cause more harm?"

Little Cock had turned his face away. "Three shillings they got for her in one of the taverns. The price of a pig. The price of a pig!"

I heard the howl of a wolf, distant, barely audible. There was no answering call. None that I heard, at least.

"They bargained for her and got the price of a pig. It came down to that. The bargaining was getting hotter and hotter so the tavern owner stepped in to suggest a price on his own much higher than anything offered. This was merely a business decision. One to prevent a fight and possible damage to his place of business, he said. It happened to him all the time and he was sick of it. He bought her himself and I have no idea who the man was. What tavern it was." He hung his head again. "There was more than one shore boat. But I couldn't have followed even if I'd wanted to."

Now came a wolf's answering call, this one much closer. A dark cloud came into my chest.

Little Cock shook his head. "I… I did something stupid."

Rabbit Woman stirred the fire again and the daytime stars rose up once more. "The wolves are singing. Sun will be going away soon. Are you warm enough, Little Cock? You're shivering again."

He ignored her question. "I was upset. I was angry. Oh! I'm only making excuses for myself, aren't I?"

"What did you do, Little Cock? What did you do?"

"I was put in irons is what I did."

"What does that—?"

"I know what it means," said Rabbit Woman. "It means you broke the law and they put chains on you. Was that on land? You could have looked for her when they let you out."

"On the ship. It was on the ship." Little Cock put his head into his hands. "It was my first taste of alcohol. Rum, it was. The curse of the seas. The reason for the slave trade. The sugar trade. Barbados, where they treat those people so badly. People like Jenteg. I've seen her kind before. We often sailed the seas of the West Indies. Dark skin, features like us. Kept as slaves. The women as… I…"

"You can't take it all onto yourself. Think of it. You were only a boy. Fourteen winters, remember? We can't keep speaking of this. You need to see this yourself. Understand it. Accept it. You were a boy!"

"I'm not a boy now."

Six

I heard him but I didn't want to so I asked Gi'gwesu to repeat what he'd just said in case I hadn't heard it right. Beside him, Jenteg clasped her hands and glanced up at him. Behind them, the snawe'g, their bright green leaves almost fully open now, swayed with a caress of the wind.

"I said, I'm going with Jenny to her land when she returns to get her daughter. We'll use her dugout. It's in excellent condition. Seaworthy."

Jenteg smiled and nodded. She had made a quick recovery from her journey and was looking even more beautiful than I thought anyone could. The trees swayed in the wind again and a pair of chickadees danced from the branch of one to another then back again.

"She's feeling much better."

Jenteg smiled and nodded again. "You're a good healer, Keskoua."

I smiled back, accepting this praise from her. "Healing comes from within. I think you know that."

"Yes, miss," she told her feet. It's strange how harsh training becomes instinct.

"She needs to get her child back from that man, her owner."

"It's too dangerous." I was now frowning at Jenteg, but her glance again sought Gi'gwesu.

As though he hadn't heard me, he kept telling me their plans. "Jenny already told me we have to be careful. She said if they see us, they will think we are runaway slaves and will capture us. She said they might capture us anyway. We will have to hide in the bush most of the time. Like she did on her journey here. It will be better for her if I go along. With two, it's easier to hide the dugout. It's heavy. I know the bush and I'm a good hunter."

"The bush is not like we know it here," came a voice from behind a stand of amasgwi'g, white birch trees. Monsieur St-Amand showed himself and approached. I wondered how long he had been hiding there. "Keskoua is right. It's too dangerous. They'll find you. That is, if you don't get swept with the tides into the open sea."

I didn't like that Monsieur St-Amand seemed to be following me around a lot more since Benny, Merit and Jacques l'Itale had showed up. He was making me more nervous than they were. Did he know something we didn't?

"Don't you have something to do at the fort?"

"There's business in Boston I should attend to. I will pay their fare. Take them on a proper ship."

Jenteg threw her arms around Gi'gwesu in a strong embrace then flew over to Monsieur St-Amand and hugged him as fiercely. "*Isso é maravilhoso!*" She hugged me the same way. "This is wonderful!"

"There's only one stipulation. No. There will be two." Monsieur St-Amand glanced over at me with something on his face like a hidden smile. Then his face went serious again as he spoke to Gi'gwesu and Jenteg. My brother's arm was around her.

"You must act as my slaves."

Jenteg took in a breath and shrugged away from Gi'gwesu.

The pair of chickadees *tsk-tsk*'ed as one from the snawe'g.

To Jenteg, Monsieur St-Amand said, "I will demand nothing of you. Especially of you, Jenteg."

Her eyes burned his for a hummingbird's wing-beat then went to her feet again. I knew that this woman had good reason not to trust slave owners, real or not. When I was spending time between her and Little Cock—her sickness from being without water and food and being under the sun of the sea for so long, even at this time of year, and his from stopping the drink—I saw the marks on her back. At first, she would not tell me how they got there, she would only let me tend to them and even this, only after a lot of asking from me. The wounds had been deep and were maybe two winters old, but I had medicines that would take some of the bumps out, maybe most of them if we could keep putting the medicines on her back every day. (I knew someone who would be more than willing to do this if I wasn't around to do it. Gi'gwesu. But she refused the offer.)

I didn't ask it but she answered my question anyway: "These scars on the outside of me are not from being a slave. They are from being thought beautiful and living beside a jealous neighbor. The scars on the inside of me are from slavery. No one can see those."

"I saw them," I told her. "I saw them when you were sitting there on the log with Hélène's shawl over your shoulders when you first got here. When Monsieur St-Amand was trying to look into your ears and your eyes with his glass instrument. The fear and anger became even stronger in you. It came out like a storm cloud."

Jenteg turned to Monsieur St-Amand. "You will demand nothing of me, you say." Her eyes began to turn from his toward the ground then she seemed to strengthen and she kept them straight on his. "Nothing? You wish me to take on my role of slave again and you call that nothing?"

Monsieur St-Amand's kind eyes swept over all three of us. "You will have to take my word during all of this. We must all cooperate to carry this off. I will be in great danger, too. I caution you: Speak no French. Above all, do not speak your Mi'gmaw language." He first put his eyes on me for four heartbeats, then on Gi'gwesu for two. "I know English. With my fair complexion, I can pass for English. Or Dutch. I speak both languages well." When I tossed him a look of surprise at this information about Dutch, he gave me that strange not-quite-a-smile again. "We can do this. There will be difficulties, of course, but—"

"What's the other…? What does that word 'stipulation' mean?"

"Condition. Agreement."

I wasn't sure I wanted to hear this either. "Then what's the other condition you want?"

"You must come along too."

My face must have showed something because Monsieur St-Amand's hand reached out to pat my shoulder in a comforting manner.

"You will have to trust me the most, Keskoua. In order to protect this woman from further anguish, I cannot have her act as my… my personal servant. You and I are friends. We will need to plan as we go each step of the way. We will all need to be able to communicate with each other. You will be with me in my cabin…" He paused and his face turned away from me. "… during the nights."

"You expect me to—!"

He turned to face me again. "No, no. It must only appear that way to the others on the ship."

"I— I don't know what to say."

"It's the only way. No one will think anything of your being with Gi'gwesu and Jenteg during the day—you will each be perceived as slaves—and this is when you will be able to communicate to them what you and I will have planned during the nights."

"It makes sense, my sister. It's a good plan."

Monsieur St-Amand motioned with his head toward Gi'gwesu. "See? He agrees."

"If we can't speak Mi'gmaw or French, how do we communicate then? It's impossible."

"Jenteg speaks English. Do you speak Dutch, too?" he asked her.

She nodded.

Conflict brushed over me like I had walked through a spider web when stepping into the bush at night to relieve myself: I wanted to push it away but at the same time I felt bad for ruining the spider's hard work, perhaps brushing away her next day's break-fast. Jacques l'Itale spoke an unknown number of languages and it seemed that our Newcomer did, too. How many more did Monsieur St-Amand speak? Ah, Monsieur St-Amand. No intricate web here to catch in your hair, but layer upon unknown layer. An onion. I wondered what I might learn about him if I peeled off his outer skin. Then the one below that. How many were there? Which one might make me cry?

"Jenteg will teach Gig English while we travel. He already knows a lot. They will be together in the slave hold anyway, so this will arouse little suspicion. You already know a great deal of English words. I can help you to learn more. Even Dutch if you wish." He looked over at Jenteg from under his eyebrows. "*E não mais Português. Compreendo?*"

"Yes. I understand," she answered in English, her smile wide.

"From here on in, until we leave, nothing but English among us. When we are together only. We don't want to raise suspicions with the so-called Benny and his gang. Agreed?"

"Agreed," we said in unison.

"At last. At long last," came another voice from the same patch of trees that Monsieur St-Amand had been waiting in. This time, it was Little Cock. "I will give you all the gold you want if only you will look for my sister while you are in Boston." He reached out to grasp Monsieur St-Amand's wrist, turned it, and dumped several gold coins into his palm.

"Ah," said Monsieur St-Amand, at first smiling as he stared at the coins. Then his face turned serious. "Wait. Not one of us has any idea what she looks like. We can't do it without you. Unless. Are you well enough to travel? After your—"

"Of course I am!" Little Cock glanced over at me and I saw the doubt in his eyes. He saw me see it and turned his face away to look at something in the bush. "Of course."

Monsieur St-Amand bounced the coins in his hand. "I'll hold onto these for now? We'll see how you're feeling as the next few days pass."

I turned Little Cock aside and we stepped several paces away from everyone. "It's very soon, you know. You will still have some of the effects for days, maybe moons to come. I—"

"I'm perfectly fine, Keskoua. Don't treat me like a child. I must find my sister."

"Even if it means putting the rest of us in danger?" I knew it wasn't fair to put this on him, but it was true. If he had one of his fits on board the ship, he might say things that would give us away. We could all be captured, Monsieur taken away to a prison for spying—which is what they would accuse him of, there was no doubt in my mind about that—and the rest of us sold as real slaves. There was no doubt in my mind about that either.

We stepped back to the group.

"I think Little Cock has something to say to you all."

He reached into the pouch hanging off his belt and took out another big handful of gold coins. These he held out to Monsieur St-Amand. "I will pay everyone's passage. I will pay for whatever you need that will get you there to find my sister. I will never be at peace. I will never be able to go on my Special Journey when my time comes unless I get her back."

Monsieur St-Amand turned to me. "Do *you* know what she looks like?"

"I was not even two winters old when they went away."

"I don't know if even I would know her," said Little Cock. "It's been twenty-six winters since I saw her and we were both—" He broke into huge sobs and I put my arms around him. "We were both children. You're right, Keskoua. I am in no shape to go anywhere. I don't know what I'm going to do when you are away. I'm afraid."

I hugged him tighter and Gig and Jenteg stepped in to put their arms around the both of us. I knew that Monsieur St-Amand wanted to join us because I saw him step forward with his arms out like a bear standing up to sniff something in the air. But he put his arms down and stepped back.

"And I know that I am thin and old now after so many years of treating myself badly. She would certainly not know who I am. I might frighten her away and lose her forever."

We released each other and him.

To me and Gi'gwesu and Jenteg he said: "I will do everything I can to help you learn about ships. And how to not do anything that will get you in trouble." At this he laughed and I hugged him again.

"So it's settled then," said Monsieur St-Amand. "We will begin our preparations."

Jenteg hugged Gi'gwesu, me, and Monsieur St-Amand again, then, after some hesitation, she hugged Little Cock, too, making him turn away from us to hide the wetness seeping up into his eyes like two springs bubbling up from the ground.

It would take a long time for Little Cock to learn what his feelings actually were and how to keep them under control. He had preserved them in rum—every one of them but anger—for over twenty-six winters. In a similar way, Jenteg was unable to hide her happiness at being able to go back to New England. I found it difficult to understand why she could be so pleased to return to the world she had escaped from, but when I reminded myself that her happiness was from having a chance to rescue her daughter from the same fate she had suffered under, I understood.

I had managed, while helping her recover from her journey, to get a little more of Jenteg's story. She had been in Boston for only a very short time, she said. That's where her new master was with her daughter. She had been sold out of Salem because of what she called "difficulties" with her master there. "He had to sell me." She refused to say why, only that Salem was a small town in New England where half the town hated the other half back. "The *whole* town hated *me*. And I won't tell you any more than that. I hope you understand?"

I didn't but I nodded anyway. "One question though?"

"Of course."

"Monsieur St-Amand says you speak Portuguese. Where did you learn Portuguese?"

"That much I will share with you."

We made ourselves comfortable. I didn't understand all the words she used but I'm good at remembering—lots of practice makes it easier—so this is pretty much what she said.

***

"Some of my ancestors came from the area of Brazil, to Barbados. I don't know if they were Arawak or if they were Carib. I think we were a mix of many peoples from many places. Over the years, there was war and fighting and of course women were taken and women were given. Languages grew and languages faded. Traditions changed. I heard it said that some of my ancestors, the Caribs, when they conquered a tribe, would take the women for wives and eat the men.

"Don't laugh, Keskoua. It's not funny. That's one of the reasons for my scars. I was accused of being a cannibal by some. A human who eats human flesh."

I must have made a face.

"No, Keskoua, I can't imagine doing that, either. It's disgusting to even think about. If it's in the blood of my ancestors, it must have missed getting into mine somehow. And I am more than happy about that.

"When the English found the island of Barbados, they set up plantations and brought many of us from the other islands and from Brazil. They brought the dark people from across the ocean, poor souls. The longest it would take for us to get from one island to another would be days or weeks—depending on the mercy of the winds—but those from across the ocean could spend months in the bottom of those stinking vessels. There was only this much space between them." Jenteg held out her hands to show the distance between the nose and tail of a gi'gwesu, a muskrat. "So many of them died.

"Secretly, we kept our language and our ways but when the dark people came, we mixed together—like your people have done here with the French. You all became Acadians, some more French than others, some pure, most not. Some of our people kept our own traditions and beliefs and our views of what the English call God, and some of the dark people kept theirs. Others joined these together.

"When Samuel Parris came to Barbados to look after his dead father's land, he bought me. I was thirteen when a hurricane came and destroyed much of Master Parris's plantation. He sold part of it, then left for Boston with me and a male Indian slave he named John. John Indian is what he named him. First they remove your identity, then they begin to work on your soul. He named me Silence. Jenteg in your language.

"In Boston, he married Elizabeth. I was glad. Him having her as a wife meant he would leave me alone most of the time and that's all I will tell you about that. At this time, I was forced to marry John Indian. He was kind to me. It was from him that I learned your language. He was from this part of the world. Imagine that. He taught me in secret. Those people believe that if anyone speaks in other than English—or... Dutch is acceptable, too—most particularly in French or Indian, it's the Devil doing it. John is—was—the father of Violet, the child I must rescue."

I wanted to hear more of her story. A lot more. I wanted to ask if John

Indian had been the one who had come part of the way in the dugout with her. But she put her lips together tight and leaned up so her face was close to mine to show me that no more words would be coming from her mouth.

I would have to wait.

Seven

To prepare for our journey, the four of us—Gi'gwesu, Jenteg, Monsieur St-Amand and I—gathered together every day on the big hill out behind the house of François and Hélène. Little Cock came along with us each time. From here, from within the trees and thick undergrowth, we had a good view of anybody coming close but they couldn't see us. We set no fire, we didn't speak until we got there in case our voices echoed.

Little Cock explained much to us about ships and sailing them and, especially, what happens when you are aboard one in a storm. That if you don't know exactly how to help, "*Exactly*, how to help!" to stay down in the hold and "try to look after anything that breaks free down there even if you're up to your neck in water."

At the first gathering, Monsieur St-Amand told us we would have to take on different names. "The name I choose will be Edward Gooden." He turned his face down like he was ashamed of something by changing his name. My people were sometimes given different names by the Grandfathers and Grandmothers as we grew up when something special happened to us or when we did something special ourselves. It was a great honor to get another name. Many of our people had been given two and sometimes three names already. Some of them younger than me. I was still waiting. I could have asked but I chose not to. Maybe when my mouth learned not to spill out everything it heard from my head, I would ask. Many times I asked my mother if I had been knocked over by a moose and hurt my head like Apalqaqamej had. And my mother would laugh and say "No. That's just you all by yourself. And that's why we all love you." And she would hug me. "But if you want to stop people from getting mad at you, you need to close this thing." She would touch my lips gently with the ends of her fingers.

"That sounds like a good name," Jenteg said to Monsieur St-Amand.

"One more thing. You must always call me Master. You may, if a situation requires it, call me Master Gooden. Never Master Edward."

"Na to'q, Monsieur St-Amand," said Gi'gwesu. "I will remember always to do—" He laughed. "This will take some practice, I think. *All right, Master.*"

We laughed but it wasn't because it was funny, it was because we knew it would be difficult.

"What will my name be?" I smiled. "Master."

Monsieur St-Amand smiled back. "Would you like to be called Dawn?"

"Of course I would. That's part of my real name: Breaking Of The Dawn."

"No it isn't," said Gi'gwesu. "And you forgot to say Master."

"Merde." I switched my crossed legs from one to the other.

"And we will not be saying merde, either. That's a sure giveaway."

"Na to'q. *Agh.* Sorry. All right. Yes, Master." I must have sounded angry or spoken too loudly, because from somewhere above, an atu'tuej threw a pine cone at me. "*Ai.* Stop that." I brushed pine cone crumbs from the top of my head.

"We must practice using each other's names from now on. Except in front of others. Especially the slave hunters. And not anywhere near Apal or Second Son. It is best only among ourselves. We need to learn to react right away when that name is called or people will become suspicious."

Gi'gwesu and I said "yes, Master" together and laughed. Jenteg said nothing and didn't laugh.

This wasn't going to be easy.

"I think Jenny is a good name for you, Jenteg. Is that acceptable? Gi'gwesu is already calling you that. And for Gi'gwesu? How about Gig? That should make things easy."

"What about me, uh, Master?" asked Little Cock. "In case I get better quickly." He looked over at me, a smile on his face. He was getting stronger and stronger every day and I hadn't seen him crying for nothing for a few days. He hadn't seen any bugs since he'd been in the cabin at Mouse Creek. At least none that he told me about.

"Ah. Little Cock. What shall we do with you?" Monsieur St-Amand turned to me. "Do you think he might be ready in time?"

"Little Cock is the only one who knows the answer to that."

Little Cock saw my look and his head went down. "I didn't tell you. I saw a bug yesterday."

"But was it really there?" Gi'gwesu reached over to rub his hand down Little Cock's back. "Maybe it was really there."

"There are no bugs like that around here. It was the size of a bobcat."

"Oh." Gi'gwesu's comforting hand rose to the back of Little Cock's neck where it paused to gently squeeze there. "What did you do?"

"I panicked. I grabbed my knife. Then screaming 'mui'n, mui'n,' bear, bear! I began to punch holes and rips in my wikuom walls." Little Cock laughed. The rest of us didn't. "Singing Bear Cub came and helped calm me down. I felt like such a fool. Bobcat and Second Son came in, too, then. Bobcat tried not to laugh when he heard what had happened. It actually made me feel a little better because I was able to see that it was kind of funny if you looked at it from outside yourself. But Second Son, as loud as he could, told me I woke his baby up and that Apal needed her sleep as she wasn't well. He threatened to banish me onto the land if I did it again."

"Who does Second Son think he is, anyway?" Gi'gwesu said. "Is he still dreaming that he should be Lnu Saqamaw?"

"Why is that?" asked Jenteg. "Why should he be Chief?"

"This is according to our traditions. He is the son of Chief. The second son."

"Hence his name," said Monsieur St-Amand.

"But traditions can be changed if they will endanger the people in any way," I told her.

"I see."

"He's nothing like his father. Or like his older brother was, either. He died trying to save a young boy from a mui'n." Gi'gwesu had never liked or trusted Second Son and he wasn't the only one of our people. "No matter what he says or does, he will never make a good chief. He thinks too much of himself. I like the one we have. And his son, Singing Bear Cub, will be a good replacement when the time comes."

Monsieur St-Amand changed seating positions and made a noise in his throat. "Shall we return to the business at hand?"

It was uncomfortable sitting on the bare ground not only for Monsieur St-Amand. We didn't dare bring anything like kaksk'ug or skins to sit on. Even if we cleared them out each time, there was too much danger that they would leave needles or hairs, or something would be left behind to show that people had been meeting there. Someone passing by might wonder what was going on and report it. Have it overheard by Jacques l'Itale and his group. We didn't even move any logs or rocks. The marks our bodies would make on the moss and the layers of last autumn's sleeping leaves would be easy to see but would look like a family of deer had rested there.

"Shall we?"

Nobody said anything for a while. We all looked around or picked at something on the bottom of our moccasins or touched our hair while Monsieur St-Amand, who was sitting there with his eyebrows still up in a question, moved his face from each of us, one to the other. He knew we were all afraid of what Second Son might do if he heard we were gathering in secret and planning something, and especially that we were doing everything we could to keep him from knowing about it. Like I said before, Second Son was quick to anger and nobody ever knew—especially him—what he might do during what Monsieur St-Amand called a rage.

"Let's give him a name, shall we?" said Monsieur St-Amand. He turned to Little Cock. "If only to make you feel as one of our crew. You are an important part of it whether you will be traveling with us or not." He turned back to the rest of us. "Yes, indeed. Let's."

We all nodded. Little Cock more firmly than the rest of us.

"What shall we name you?" Then Monsieur St-Amand asked Jenteg, "Will we be among Puritans?"

Her frightened eyes turned quickly to me with a question in them: *Did you tell him about me?*

I had not.

"Yes. My daughter is among them."

"In that case, we will name one of you with a Puritan name and since you are the last one, Little Cock, it shall be you."

Little Cock's eyes went wide and he glanced around at the rest of us.

"The Puritans are a very strict lot," said Monsieur St-Amand. "They make our priests look excessively permissive. They name their children with either sins or virtues. 'Silence,' for instance. Strange folks. Now let me see. What shall we call you? Pride, Greed, Lust, Anger, Gluttony. Gluttony… Hmm. No. That's the old you, isn't it?" Monsieur St-Amand's smile was kind. "How about Humility… Mercy? Temperance.

Courage… Perseverance. Which of these do you prefer?"

Little Cock looked around at us, hoping we'd help him decide. I didn't know what most of these words meant.

"I think Perseverance would be good," said Monsieur St-Amand. "Most suitable, in fact, after what you have been through for love."

This made Little Cock frown.

"The love of your sister. And it means determined."

This made Little Cock smile.

"We can call you Pierce for short. How's that?"

Little Cock shrugged and looked around again at the rest of us.

"Shortening the names is common practice. In fact, sometimes quite necessary. I once met a man named Nick whose real name was Born Of Fornication."

Jenny and Little Cock laughed but Gi'gwesu and I didn't understand.

Jenny whispered to Gi'gwesu loud enough for me to hear: "I'll explain later."

"I will accept Pierce. May I practice, too? Master?"

Monsieur St-Amand reached over and patted Little Cock's shoulder.

"Of course, you may. Now we must consider wardrobe. Dawn, because you will be my personal slave, you must dress in the Puritan manner."

"With all those aprons and collars and cloth upon cloth around me?" I think my nose must have wrinkled or something. No. I know it did. I couldn't help it.

Monsieur St-Am—"Master"—looked hard at me from under his eyebrows.

"Na to'q, na t— *Agh.* All right. I'll ask Marguerite what I can borrow from her. She likes things from New England. She's always sending Claude to the port with a list."

Monsieur St-Amand raised his eyebrows and put his hand out in a gesture that meant he required something else from me.

All this was going to take me more than practice. I would have to teach myself to look up at the world without looking up, from the bottom of deep, dark hole full of chenoos. "Master." And I managed to say this while looking at him and my feet at the same time. And without laughing.

"That's better."

So every day we practiced the many things that were difficult for Gi'gwesu, Little Cock and me like looking at our feet when we spoke to Monsieur St-Am—to Master. Each time we met, we brought a small amount of clothing and supplies with us. These, Monsieur St-Amand would bring—a little at a time—to his surgeon's office at the fort, to be hidden away there until the time came when we would all be putting on our act. We spoke only English. (I was learning a lot of new words.) We practiced wearing Newcomers' clothing and shoes. Shoes! Shoes hurt. They made Gi'gwesu and me trip over everything, even over the flat wooden floor in the cabin at Mouse Ridge where we sometimes practiced walking. We kept Jenny carefully hidden.

Eight

One day, Benny wanted to hold what he called a big meeting at The Bear around a sacred fire like we did whenever we needed to talk about something that would affect everybody in the village. I don't know how he learned about our ceremonies. What he did know he was mixed up about.

When Newcomers first arrived here—not all of them, but some, especially those like Benny—they would be reading out of a book and talking to their wives and children and other Newcomers and their children while pointing at things—even us, sometimes: "See that tree? Bears like to eat the bark on it. You can tell because they scratch it off to chew on it. This is an Indian savage and if you don't act important around them, keep them afraid of you and respecting you—like you train a dog—they will scalp you and eat your heart. They eat hearts raw. They put people's brains in their soup and cook pelts in it to eat when they go on what they call their… Let me see." And this man would run his finger down the page of his book and say, "Ah, yes. Their Special Journeys. We must be careful around them. Dangerous godless savages."

At the beginning, it was all we could do to keep from laughing in their faces but got to know that these new people would soon learn that there was little truth in what they read in books written by people who had never even been out of their own village in the land of their Kings. So we felt sorry for Benny and at first we were going to go along with him and have all of us go to his meeting to see what he had to say. But when he said that only men were allowed to be at meetings, "no women, no children," Lnu Saqamaw, Chief, told him he would then have to have his meeting at the tavern in the fort, in that case.

"That's where White men have their meetings," Lnu Saqamaw told him. "Go there. It's full of men."

I don't think Benny, tough as he acted around us, would want to be having a meeting in English in a room full of drunken French men, most of them soldiers, enemies. He declared that he would have his meeting in the clearing near Père Bigaud's church. Père Gaëtan was no longer with us. He had done good work with us here so his chief had given him what he called "a promotion" and made him go to the settlement at Québec to train Fathers there. We all cried when he left, even him. Père Bigaud was also a kind man but old and shaky and didn't say much even in his talks during the Mass. I think he believed in our ways more than in the ways of the Fathers. That's why I liked and trusted him.

Père Bigaud told me quietly: "At first I thought, just for the hell of it, I would tell them they could have their meeting in the church. That there were many seats. Even a special raised platform in a corner for this Benny person to speak from. And I meant the pulpit." One side of Père Bigaud's mouth smiled as he closed one eye at me. We both laughed. "I would have enjoyed seeing their heads explode and their eyes pop out just *thinking* about being inside a Catholic church, the Devil's lair."

"I would have liked to be a ga'qaquj in a tree for that one, a crow."

"They refused the offer of my home. One look at the crucifix on the wall and that one with the big muscles ran, almost screaming, out of there."

I laughed hard at this one.

"So I set them up in the far corner of the grounds. I think you know the one I mean."

I knew. "The one closest to the swamp."

"The very corner." Père Bigaud could not hold in his laugh.

"Where the glmuej are thickest."

"The very corner. They are so thick there this time of year, I can hear their infernal *ziizzziiz* from inside the church itself."

***

Singing Bear Cub and Bobcat came to me (their skin smelling strongly of mint) right after Benny's meeting to tell me what had gone on. These young men were already very important to our community and had done their best to learn both French and English at every opportunity so had understood every word spoken.

Imitating Benny, even pushing his stomach out and lifting his head high, Singing Bear Cub repeated: "Unfortunately, we were not able to have our meeting in the normal meeting place of these people, but I repeat: It's not possible for women and children to contribute anything of value toward our discussions."

Bobcat laughed. "It's really true, Keskoua. The guy said it. And he made J-B leave."

"Was Claude there? And he didn't protest?"

Bobcat nodded yes then shook his head no. "J-B left then circled around and listened from inside the trees. Right behind them. We could all see him but *they* couldn't see him."

Singing Bear Cub laughed. "And every time one of those guys slapped at a glmuej, J-B made a motion that he had terrible pain on his own body in the same spot."

"It was all we could do not to give him away by laughing. Gi'gwesu had to leave."

I looked past them to see if anyone else was coming along the path. "Did Falcon go to my mother's wikuom by another path?"

"He wasn't there," said Bobcat. "Said he wasn't about to give any respect to those men by attending. And besides, Second Son was acting up again, running around trying to collect what he was calling 'an army' to fight les Maudits anglais. Falcon went to look for him, wanting to calm him down before he did something stupid and get hurt. Or worse."

"He doesn't need an army to fight Benny and Jacques l'Itale and that man with the big muscles."

"The man with the muscles is called Merit. And Second Son didn't mean *them*," said Singing Bear Cub. "He wants to take on the whole of New England. Wipe out every English man and woman within travel distance. He wants us to go the Big Meadow and buy a ship from one of the fellows there."

"Oh, not that again. He still believes that everyone should follow *him* instead of Lnu Saqamaw. And make war."

"He does."

No Falcon. No Gi'gwesu. I would have to rely on the words of these young men to tell me what Benny had discussed at his meeting.

"What did that wolverine have to say anyway? Why a big meeting?"

Singing Bear Cub began. "He said he was hunting for an escaped slave and was having a great deal of trouble finding her. She murdered her husband so we should be more than happy to help him and his men find her because the dead husband was one of us. A Mi'gmaw man."

"I didn't believe him," said Bobcat.

"He wants us to take him to every corner in our area and even go to Mirligueche with him—"

"Mirligueche?"

"He *said* she might have gone there to see if there were any ships ready for battle."

I didn't believe that, either.

"He said she was a spy."

"Takes one to know one, e'e?" said Bobcat.

"He said he would not rest until he had examined all of our land. Said he was particularly interested in seeing the wheat fields in the Big Meadow."

"Ah," I said while thinking at the same time: The Big Meadow again? Did Second Son know more than he realized he knew? What was so important about the Big Meadow? Was it the ships they built there? Or the food they grew? In the past, the English had often tried to break down the dikes that held back the sea from the land that grew the wheat for most of Acadia. For much of New England, too.

"And he also showed an interest—I'm sure it was flattery—in our ways of fighting."

"What is this word 'flattery'?"

"They make you feel good when they lie to you," said Bobcat.

"Ah," I said while thinking once again at the same time: These men, this Benny, this Merit, this Jacques l'Itale are much more than slave hunters.

"If he wasn't quite so English, Benny would get a lot of information out of Second Son, wouldn't he?"

Yes. Second Son would give him this information without a thought. Only to be thought of as important if only for the moment. I was getting worried now.

As though Singing Bear Cub had been right inside my head listening to me think, he said, "Our beautiful Newcomer with the dark skin is not the enemy. She is no spy. First he claims to be a slave hunter. Then a spy hunter. Then he wants to examine the wheat fields of the Big Meadow? What is he now? A farmer? We can't trust him. This mi'jan is far more than we realize. I just know it."

"I agree," I said. "But we can't give ourselves away by letting him know we know."

From close to the swamp where Benny's meeting had taken place, a pair of huge wings rose up. A tmgwalignej, a heron. I always wondered how those things could fly.

"Four of our people are willing to take him to the Big Meadow and show him around." The fierceness on Bobcat's face told me why the Grandfathers had given him his name. "Claude said he'd take him to Mirligueche instead."

I trusted Claude enough to know that he would make the journey to Mirligueche as long and as difficult as possible, perhaps even getting lost several times along the way.

I wondered who the four people were who had been willing to betray our friends at the Big Meadow. Lose the Big Meadow to the English, lose the whole of Acadia.

***

I had my own gathering with Marguerite, Falcon, my mother, Rabbit Woman, and Hélène. I needed to decide who I was going to trust my sons, Tities and Nalagit, and my daughter, Su'n, with. Tities was ten winters old and Su'n was eight but not old enough to take responsibilities for her two-year-old brother, Nalagit. Nalagit was no longer suckling so he wouldn't miss me for that, but would miss me in many other ways. I was very worried about what might happen to them and to Marguerite (whose baby was coming in two moons) if the voyage took as long as Little Cock said it could take. Sometimes it took two or three weeks to move along the coast, he told us. Sometimes months if the winds and the tides were against you. You could sometimes be within sight of your destination and have the winds and the tides play their tricks on you and move you far away again. This would be both going and coming back. We would not leave on a Friday, he said. Absolutely not. He said he didn't really understand why not, but as far as he knew, no ship would sail on a Friday. Some captains would not sail on a Thursday, either.

I trusted Hélène with my life but I didn't trust her not to put her Newcomer and Fatherly ideas into my children's heads. She was always trying. But not on purpose. Not really. It was because these ideas were so strong inside her, she didn't know there was anything different anymore. And of course, she wanted to please her husband, François. The Fathers had told her she had to do what François said or they'd both go to Hell.

I trusted Marguerite and Claude. They had treated my daughter, Jeanne, with deep love and with respect for the ways of our people and theirs, too. Somehow, they were able to put the two ways together and end up with something even better for her. But Marguerite and Claude had nine of their own to look after: two from Marguerite's first husband; my Jeanne; six from Claude and now another one coming up. The last baby Marguerite had was harder coming out because it was a big one. She was carrying this one the same way, sticking out farther in front. I didn't want to put more work on her. Rabbit Woman had been with me when Marguerite had Josephe, the big baby girl, so she knew what to do if it was a big one again, or even if it came out backwards like one of the other ones did.

Falcon and my mother and I decided that my mother would be the best one to look after my children even though she was getting frailer now. Not frailer because she was old—her mind was really good—but because she had a bad fall down some rocks at the shore the spring after Gi'gwesu was born. She was climbing down to help my father who fell down first. She hurt her back, both her legs and one arm. She was lucky somebody found her before all the blood drained out of her arm. My father wasn't lucky. She never took another man after him but many wanted her.

My sister had four children and helped Giju', Mother, whenever she came to visit but she had married out so had already been and gone back to Mirligueche. There would not be enough time to have even Little Cock go fetch her. But Falcon was good to help with anything. There wasn't much he couldn't do himself. So my husband and my little ones would be taken care of by my mother and my mother would be taken care of by them. I had no reason to worry there. But I knew I would miss them terribly.

***

The next morning, we were in the middle of moving the children's clothes over, and some skins and fresh kaksk'ug, when my mother called me outside the wikuom to talk to me. "Over here," she said, and led me into the bushes out of hearing range of everybody.

"What is it, Giju'? You look worried. Is it because I'm leaving?"

"Apal came to talk to me this morning."

My heart reached up to catch hold of the back of my tongue.

"She knows something's going on. She was in a rage. Do you want to tell me about this new woman taking all the men away?"

"She's not— Oh, Giju', not you, too. She can't help it if she's beautiful."

"So she is then?"

"Is what?"

My mother's eyes looked into mine so deep I think she could see where my braids were parted at the back of my head. "She's very, very beautiful, isn't she?"

I nodded.

My mother laughed. "You want her gone quick, too, don't you?"

My mother knew me well. "Yes. But not for *that* reason."

"And what reason would *that* one be, tutji'j, little daughter?"

"I trust Falcon. He loves me. I don't trust Apal though. What did you tell her?"

Giju' had told Apal that she'd talk to me and see what I knew about the situation. That seemed to settle Apal down but it wouldn't last for long. Giju' and I both knew that.

"And she's not the only one who's angry. Do you want to know who else came to me about this woman?"

I didn't but my mother was going to tell me anyway.

"Marguerite's cousin."

"Which one?"

"I don't know which one. They all look the same to me. They never come around the village, just stick to their own. They even take the long way around to get to and from the fort. Why should I try to learn their names? They don't know mine. They don't want to."

To tell you the truth, Giju' was right about that.

"It's the one who's always following Mathieu around. You know the one."

"Oh, her. Yes. She is called Charlotte. What's her problem? Mathieu wouldn't dare look at another woman."

"He looked at this one. This Newcomer. Remember, tutji'j? He's the one who found her."

"Claude and One-Eyed Joe found her, too."

"The way this cousin talks, you'd think he'd had her hidden away in a cabin back in the bush and got caught with her by them. She wants her gone and is threatening to tell Jacques l'Itale."

"That's not good."

"I don't like that you're involved in all this but you are old enough to know what you're doing. I hope you are anyway." My mother held me close and kissed my cheek several times. I thought she wasn't going to let me go.

To tell you the truth again, I wasn't so sure it was going to turn out the way we saw it happening in our heads. We hadn't even left yet and it was getting complicated already. Perhaps too dangerous.

"I have to go talk to Monsieur St-Amand about this." I pulled myself away from my mother and started away.

"Marguerite doesn't want her around, either, you know. She—"

I stopped and turned back to my mother. "She what, Giju'? What did she do?"

"The gathering was held at her house."

"Gathering?"

"Yes. Marguerite's sisters. That cousin. Two other cousins, I think, too. Some of our women. Apal. Her baby is doing really well, tutji'j, but she isn't. She is getting thinner and thinner even though she eats well. Maybe you shouldn't go. People need you."

"Don't change the subject, Giju'. What gathering?"

"We all decided we'd tell those men she was here and they would take—"

"*WE?*" I couldn't believe my ears. "*We*, Giju'? We? You were there and you didn't tell me? You didn't tell me about it? That you were going? I can't believe it. I cannot believe it. My own mother putting me in danger."

"*You* in danger? How could you be in danger if they take her away from here? She's best gone. She's causing trouble. More trouble than any Newcomer ever caused."

"I can't believe it. Giju'! I am in danger because I will be protecting this woman and you agreed to send these men after her. Which is against me."

"Why would you want to protect her, Keskoua? Why?"

"I'm a healer, Giju'."

"You did your part. You helped her heal. She is well now. What part of healing calls for going away on a ship, leaving your own children behind, risking your life for this… this troublemaker?"

"You don't know then."

"Know what?"

"Gi'gwesu hasn't told you?"

"Told me what?"

"Love is making him follow her."

"Gi'gwesu is going?"

"He thinks if he goes with her and helps her find her child she will fall in love with him."

"And you say this woman does not cause trouble?"

I turned and walked away. I had to find Monsieur St-Amand. Tell him we had to leave immediately.

Nine

I didn't dare run straight to Monsieur St-Amand. That would have made people pay attention and maybe follow me just to see what I was up to. Our small group had enough problems without that. So I walked along acting as if I had nothing else to do but enjoy the new growth coming up along the sides of the path and watch the birds flying to and from their nests feeding their new babies or building nests or still choosing mates. But I enjoyed it fast. No matter where you went near our village, there was always somebody going the other way or the same way for a short distance, but today, each time I turned into a new path, I could feel that somebody behind me was going the exact same way. I didn't like this. I came to a sharp turn in the path, went around it, then stepped into the bush behind a wide tree.

It was J-B. He came around the corner in the path and stopped, frowned, looked left then right (where I was), looked down at the plants—the plants that had been crushed by my moccasins—and stepped up to my tree and tipped his head sideways to look around it. "What's the matter, Keskoua? You hiding from a chenoo or something?"

I came out of my hiding place and back onto the path. We both looked around us and listened for a short while before anyone spoke.

"I have a message from Little Cock," he whispered.

He was a tall boy so I didn't have to bend down too far to listen.

"He heard those slave hunter men talking. They're not slave hunters. They got paid to find her so they're going to do that. But they're going to kill her and just bring back her scalp. They don't want to be bothered with her. They have… Hmm. How did Little Cock say it?" J-B scratched his chin. "Ah, yes. He told me: 'No. They are not slave hunters. Look at him. That Benny. He's somebody important. Look at the way l'Itale and that fellow, Merit—especially Merit—act around him. They fear him. He has some kind of authority over them.' They are seeking information. About us." J-B looked around at the bush and this made me look around again, too. "He said to tell you he heard Merit call that Benny guy 'major.' Major church. What does that mean, major church? I don't understand English. English words don't want to stay in my head."

I wasn't sure what 'major church' meant either but I didn't like it. "I don't know. Grande église, maybe? He's certainly big as a church."

This brought a small smile to J-B's worried face. "Little Cock said Benny told l'Itale to go to François's house and look for that… he called her a bad word… for the lady there. He had something else for Merit to do, but Little Cock couldn't hear what."

"Where's Little Cock now?"

"He ran away somewhere."

"Oh, J-B. I don't want to put you in any kind of danger. But please, run as fast as you can to warn François that l'Itale is on his way. Be careful. These are—"

"I know. I know. They're bad men. That's where I was going but I saw you first. To tell François. I'll be careful. Don't worry. And I know a short cut. You're not the only one I follow around, you know."

I made my eyebrows ask him a question.

"One of Little Cock's shortcuts is right up here." J-B grinned, ran a few paces then as quietly as an owl in flight, he disappeared into the bush.

***

Little Cock, even in his weakened state, had arrived at the house of François and Hélène and was already hiding and peering in through a back window long before young, long-legged J-B arrived to tell them that Jacques l'Itale was on his way.

"And where did you hear this information?" François asked J-B. "You don't understand English."

"Little Cock told me."

"And you are going to believe that lying pisspot?"

"Of course I am. Jenteg. Jenteg. Where are you? You have to get away." J-B glanced into the children's bedroom then opened the door to the other bedroom and peered in. "Where is she?"

"*Fermez cette porte!*" came Hélène's shrill, startled voice.

"Sorry," he told her, smiling, his eyes bright as he turned back to look around the main room again.

Little Cock heard someone approaching the front of the house at the exact same time as one of the floorboards near the dining table moved upwards.

"I'm here," Jenteg said as she climbed out of her hiding place.

François hushed her with a "tais-toi" as he helped her climb out of the hole under the floor. "Allez, allez, the both of you."

As she and J-B scooted out the back door of the house, Little Cock stopped them. "Come this way," he whispered, leading them into a thick stand of evergreens. "Now stay here. Don't talk. Don't move."

With one arm around J-B, Jenteg, eyes wide, nodded.

"You may watch and listen through the branches, but... I don't need to say more, do I?"

J-B and Jenny shook their heads in unison.

"If they don't manage to control the situation inside, you'll know soon enough. If that's the case, then you, Jenny, must go hide out in the secret place up the hill. And you, young man, must play the part of a snipe mama:

lead l'Itale away on a false chase. Na t'oq?"

"Na t'oq."

Little Cock returned to the house to peer once again through the back window, this time using only the corner of an eye between the curtains.

Jacques l'Itale was already inside having burst through the thick wooden front door. He pointed his musket upward while Hélène dragged her sons Georges and Ti-To around behind her. Slowly, moving only her feet, she travelled smoothly toward the stove where a coffee pot bubbled and an iron frying pan sizzled with eggs and meat. From his viewpoint at the window, Little Cock made note that there was no baby basket. The wee girl must have been asleep in the children's room.

The floorboards had been replaced over Jenny's hiding place but there was a small dusting of earth on the floor there. Would l'Itale see it?

François took a sideways step toward his wife and boys and this prompted an outburst from l'Itale. "Don't move. Both of you stay where you are. Stop moving!" He pointed the musket at Hélène.

She gasped.

François: "Don't."

Jacques l'Itale's left hand pulled a pistol from his belt. He cocked it. Fired it into the floor a pace away from François's feet, two paces away from the spot of earth and Jenny's hiding spot.

From the children's room came the cry of a rudely awakened baby.

Jacques l'Itale returned the pistol into his belt and drew another from behind his back.

François moved another step but this time, farther away from his family.

The baby's cries increased in loudness.

"Shut the baby up," Jacques l'Itale demanded, motioning toward the children's room with his musket.

Hélène shuffled the boys ahead of her as she started toward the children's open door. On the way past the stove, she pushed the boys toward their room, leaped back to pick up the iron frying pan from the stove. Overcooked eggs and fried meat went everywhere as she raised it into the air with both hands. With all her strength, she brought it down onto the back of Jacques l'Itale's head.

He crumpled.

Little Cock ran into the house and together, he, François and Hélène dragged the limp l'Itale outside and lifted him up onto a cart beside the shed. Hélène, spattered with fried food and with burn blisters rising on her hands, began to cover him with an old sailcloth from inside the shed. Jenny rushed over to help Hélène smooth the cloth over Jacques l'Itale's still form.

"Is he dead?" asked J-B bending close and lifting a corner of the sailcloth to peer underneath.

"I don't think so," said Hélène, "but I would not shed a tear if he was." She pulled a corner of the sailcloth smooth over Jacques l'Itale's projecting foot. "Mind you, I would not laugh either."

"Oui," J-B said. "We will be in grande difficulté, big trouble, if he's dead. C'est-à-dire, that is to say, if anybody finds out we did it. Especially that Maudit anglais Benny."

"Mon Dieu," said Hélène. "You are sounding more and more like your mama and papa every day." She turned to kiss François's cheek. "Soyez prudent, mon cher mari. Soyez prudent."

François put his back end to the cart and hoisted up its handles. Either out of breath, or greatly worried—Little Cock told me he wasn't sure which—he gasped out "I'll take him to the foot of The Bear. I'll display him there. Make it look like he was climbing and fell. The rest of you, go do what you have to do. Allez-vous en. Vite, vite." Hauling the cart behind him, he started away toward the front of the house. "Must I tell you that none of this happened? That he was never here?"

"I'll caution the boys." Hélène went into the house.

To J-B, Little Cock said "Find Gi'gwesu. Tell him to go to the fort. To the surgeon's office. Understand?"

"Oui. Je comprend."

"Then go tell your papa that he must distract Benny and Merit."

"Je comprend."

"Then find Keskoua. Tell her to pretend to be ill or injured and to get to the surgeon's office at the fort. We can't have everyone showing up there without reason."

"Je comprend."

"Then run ahead of Keskoua to alert Monsieur St-Amand that he will be needing to 'pack the trunk.' Immediately."

"Oui," and off he went.

To Hélène, who had returned from inside the house, "I need a barrel. An empty one. Best would be a whisky barrel. They're a good size. Do you have one by any chance?"

"I do," she said. "In the children's room."

Little Cock followed her back into the house. The boys were sitting at the table eating bread.

"It serves as a side table in here," she said leading him into the room where it sat between two high cots. The baby was once more sleeping. "François found it in the bush behind Père Bigaud's a few years ago." She began removing toys and books from the top of it to place them on the narrow beds. "He found it in that infernal swamp of his. Can you imagine? I have no idea how it got there."

"I do," Little Cock admitted quietly to no one in particular.

They rolled the heavy barrel to the bedroom doorway then uprighted it to rock it through, rolled it again, then rocked it outside.

"Here we are, Miss Jenny. Prepare yourself to get folded into a barrel."

"Are you certain you can do this on your own, Little Cock?" asked Hélène. "It's going to be even heavier with her inside."

To Hélène he said, "Blankets. I need blankets to protect Jenny from injury. I will have to roll the barrel all the way to the port. Then up the gangplank onto a ship. Do you have enough confidence in me, Jenny?"

"No, no," Hélène protested. "No amount of blankets will protect her from being rolled around in a barrel for that length of time. There's an old travois behind the shed. I'll get new rope for it." She disappeared into the house again, then immediately stuck her head out the doorway. "Or should we wait for François to return with the cart? That would make it much easier."

"A cart would create too much suspicion. I don't own one. Someone might assume I stole it. A travois will work well." He pushed Jenny toward the back of the shed. "Get the travois. I'll prepare the barrel."

"Travois? I don't know this word."

"Two long poles roped together."

She disappeared around behind the shed. Her voice came back: "Yes. It's here."

"Hélène says it needs to be restrung. Does it?" With his hunting knife, Little Cock pried the top ring from the barrel to release the cover. "Think you can figure out how to do that?"

"All I need is rope and a knife. Two of the most important objects in the world, don't you agree?" Her laughter bounced off the bush to dance into Little Cock's ears. "Separately or together."

Little Cock was beginning to like this Newcomer not only for her looks. She was a strong woman both mentally and physically it seemed.

Ten

I was almost at the fort when J-B caught up to me. "J-B! Already. You are either a very fast runner or you know a lot more shortcuts than I thought you did."

"Both. But there's no time to talk about that. Quick. Damoiselle Autoritaire and her beau, Mathieu, are almost upon us. Fake a limp."

"What?"

"Fake a limp. You need to see the surgeon at the fort for it. Right?" He closed one eye.

"Ah."

Just then, Charlotte and Mathieu came up behind us.

"Bonjour, Keskoua. Comment ça va?"

I took a few steps along the path with my left foot curled inward. This caused a convincing limp. "I am well. Thank you. But I seem to have done something to my foot."

"So I see," said Charlotte, known as Damoiselle Autoritaire to J-B and no doubt to his papa which is where J-B would have heard it. "What did I say, Mathieu? It's that woman, I tell you. I've heard about women like her. She is bedeviled. She causes illnesses and misfortune to all who cross her path. She will bedevil all of us. Look at Keskoua there and all she did was use her heathen ways to help that ungodly creature."

"And how are *you*, this lovely day, Charlotte?" I didn't even try to keep the arrows out of my voice. "I am going to see your countryman the surgeon at the fort about my bedeviled condition. Do you think he might have any un-heathen medicines in his quarters?"

"Pah," she said and continued on her way but not without tossing more of her opinion back. "I don't know what he sees in you people and your ways. Honnête à Dieu, I don't see it. Especially what he sees in you, Keskoua. There must be something going on between you two. Cela me donne la chair de poule. In actual fact, it gives me more than the willies merely thinking of his hands on you and then on me. A White surgeon should be for White people only. There's no telling what kind of diseases or bugs you people have on you. Lice and… *eee*. I don't even want to think about it."

Obviously holding in a laugh, J-B looked up expecting a returning volley from me. When none came he opened his own mouth. "I'll not have you speaking to Maman and Papa's friend in that manner, ma cousine au second degré. Ce n'est pas poli, not polite at all."

J-B certainly took after his mother when it came to speaking his mind and after his father when it came to protecting women.

"Your mother will hear about this rudeness, young man."

"I certainly hope so," he fired back. "And it had better be the truth, too."

At this, Mathieu put his arm across Charlotte's shoulders to turn her in the direction of the fort and thus away on their intended errands.

"That foot of hers is bedeviled, I tell you."

"Oui, ma chérie. Oui. Come along now. We have a lot to do and I don't want to be returning home in the dark." And he turned back to me with an apologetic smile.

***

Little Cock and Jenteg moved quickly along some of Little Cock's shortcuts through the bush and took turns with the travois. They made good time that way and were soon close enough to the fort to be seen or heard so Little Cock helped her into the barrel.

Before he put the cover back on, he asked. "You sure you'll be all right with this?"

"I've spent thc last fcw days buried under a floor, haven't I? This at least smells better."

"I quite like you," said Little Cock. "I wish you good weather and that you complete your task without trouble. He slid the cover over her upturned face, then fitted the iron hoop around the top of the barrel. "Time to weigh anchor and hoist the mizzen! Off we go into the unknown future."

To get to the docks, Little Cock had to pass the fort. He was almost past when a "lapointe" holding a musket across his chest stepped in his way. "Who are you?" asked the guard. "And where do you think you're going with that barrel?"

To Little Cock, one soldier looked the same as any other because he had never faced any of them directly for fear of being recognized as one of the two accused of killing his own captain, but this one seemed to know him.

"Oh, it's you, Little Bird. I *heard* you were out of your mind or some such. I guess you need to take that barre—"

"I was. I was."

"You need to take that barrel to where it came from, sir. I'm sorry, but we can't have you wandering around tout fou, all crazy like."

"I'm not crazy. And I *am* taking it back where it came from, sir." This time, Little Cock made eye contact. "I believe, since I stole it off a ship, I will return it to a ship. Does that sound fair and honest and Christ-like to you, sir?"

"It does but I am obliged to ask, since you are heading for the docks:

What is *in* your barrel there?"

"Something dark, beautiful and wished for from Barbados."

"Ah, oui. Le rhum est très bon, rum is wonderful. But sir, have you noticed?" he waved his musket at the barrel. It says whisky. It's written right there."

Little Cock pretended to study sections of the barrel and in the process, turned the open bung hole away from the soldier. This lapointe was a sharp one.

"Now that I have stopped drinking this swill, I have become a changed man. I've decided it's time I made amends for some of the sins I committed while under the influence of this devilish substance. I am starting with the return of this barrel of drink—whatever it is, whether rum or whisky."

"Looks like an old barrel. The contents must be very old, too."

"I'd say maybe twenty-three, twenty-four years old."

"That old, hè?"

"I hid it when I was drunk and forgot about it."

The lapointe threw back his head to let out a mocking laugh. "If it is so well-aged and dark and beautiful, perhaps you should sell it to the crew on the brigantine. That ship is so new, it could use some good luck with something old on it."

"Right you are." Little Cock threw back his own head and laughed, too. "A new ship you say? Cargo or passenger?"

"Could be either, I suppose, now that you ask," said the soldier. "I'm always suspicious of those ships that are built for speed. Too many pirates get hold of them. Maybe that's why."

"Yes. Yes. Damned pirates. Always stealing ships. Dirty bâtards."

"She hasn't even been blessed yet I heard. Makes me even more suspicious about her. This little ship has no name, no registration. Nothing. I heard the owner lives at Big Meadow. Builds ships there. He's not a pirate then. But my suspicion is that he built this particular one for pirates."

"Is the captain on board?"

"The builder is the owner is the captain. One and the very same. High opinion of himself, I'd say." That mocking laugh again. "Very suspicious."

"I see."

Little Cock bent over to put his weight behind the barrel to move it.

"Halt!" Another voice, this one appallingly familiar to Little Cock. "And just where do you think you're going, gtigiewinuj, drunkard?"

It was Second Son.

"I'm off to mind my own affairs, what about you?"

Attempting to stand up straight and proud, Second Son staggered.

"What's with you?" Little Cock asked, genuinely concerned. "Have you been…? You have. You damn fool."

"Needed to take the edge off. Apal is sick."

"I know. Everybody knows."

"Really sick and I can't find Keskoua."

"Then ask Rabbit Woman." Little Cock turned away and pushed the barrel for two rolls. He felt Second Son's hand on his shoulder, smelled the drink off him. It brought back memories both good and bad.

"I don't trust her."

Little Cock turned to face Second Son. "Why not? She's every bit as good as Keskoua."

"That's not why. It's because her husband hates me."

"With good reason but she would never—"

Second Son turned to the soldier. "I demand to see the surgeon. My woman needs him. I can't wake her up. She's cold and stiff. Her baby—my son—won't stop crying. He's hungry."

The soldier's haughty laugh rang off the fort's high gate as he turned to pull it open. “I’m surprised you Indians don’t know what the symptoms of dead are. Even I know them. Go ahead. Make a fool of yourself. But leave that bottle here.”

Little Cock hadn’t noticed but the legging on Second Son’s right leg bulged with the shape of a bottle.

“What bottle?” said Second Son, puffing himself up and turning away from the soldier slightly.

Bringing his musket down by the length of a blue jay’s wing, the soldier took a step closer to Second Son. Second Son jumped forward to knock the musket out of the soldier’s hands. It went flying into the air to bounce off the edge of the open gate into the fort. The sound of metal against the iron hinge at the gate’s edge alerted two men inside.

As Second Son leaped onto the soldier, the two men rushed out of the fort to assist their fellow.

Little Cock took the opportunity to roll the barrel away. “Brace yourself in there. I must be quick about this before more lapointes come and think I’m part of that mêlée. We’ve made it this far, we cannot fail now.”

“Agreed. *Ai.*” An uncomfortable and broken laugh came from the barrel along with Jenteg’s jerky words. “*Querido Deus no céu*, dear God in heaven. *Ai.* Hurry, Little Cock. *Ai.* Hurry.”

Yes. Little Cock was liking this woman more and more.

Eleven

When Little Cock flashed a few gold coins under the nose of Willem KrommeZee, the ship's builder, there was no longer any question: KrommeZee's brigantine would be sailing, unblessed, unnamed, unregistered. She was a beauty. So newly built she still smelled of sawdust. She would be fast with that long bowsprit.

"I know it's Friday, but it must be today," Little Cock told Willem KrommeZee. "It must be."

"I see no problem with that. We're almost ready to set sail. What's so important about Friday?"

Behind Willem KrommeZee, the five men who were securing what appeared to be the last of twelve guns stopped what they were doing to glance over. One of them, a large man with a terribly scarred face, frowned when his eyes met those of Little Cock.

Little Cock turned back to KrommeZee. "Are you certain you know how to sail this beautiful lady, uh, Captain? You seem to know nothing of the rules of the sea. 'Never set sail on a Friday.' This tells me you are new to captaining."

"Superstition and balderdash," KrommeZee replied, making a grand gesture with his arm at the crew. "Right men? I got her from Grand-Pré to here, didn't I? And we set out on the first Monday in April, too! Didn't we?" He turned to Little Cock. "Another bad day according to you lot, yes?" Back to his men. "Well? Did I not get her here safely?"

As one and without expression on any face: "Yes, Captain."

He leaned in close to Little Cock. "You are making yourself sound like a pirate."

"Can you do it or not?"

A loud shout from the ship forward to Captain KrommeZee's caused Little Cock to glance over. Another shout, and on the other ship—a large, three-masted cargo ship—a crew member pointed upward. "*She's not secure yet. Belay that.*"

Another man cried out: "*BACK OFF!*"

Two men were up at the yardarm and the one they were shouting at was about to crawl out onto it. The second man aloft was pointing at the rigging and calling out in a language Little Cock didn't understand.

"Damn fool," said Captain KrommeZee.

"What's the problem?" asked Little Cock. "Looks stable enough."

The man crawled out farther. The second man scurried down the rigging like a spider after prey. He looked up, shook his head and made the Sign of the Cross.

"It's not. They're just finishing up repairs. Cannon fire damaged some of the rigging. Bloody pirates! Like the men are saying, it's not secured yet. See?"

Try as he might, Little Cock could see nothing out of the ordinary.

"The yardarm. What an idiot. Can he not feel that?"

"Feel what?"

"Look at the angle of the yardarm. His weight on it is making it tilt. The rigging's coming loose. Ah. There it goes."

Little Cock saw it now. Instinct made him cry out along with several of the crew from both ships as three of the ropes let go and the yardarm took on a more-pronounced angle. "*Get away. Get off. It's coming apart. GET OFF THERE!*"

The man on the yardarm froze. Slowly, he attempted to move back to the mainmast but it was too late. Ropes screamed as the yardarm dipped farther and the man slid all the way along it to its tip, his hands grabbing for rigging but unsuccessfully. Down he floated. If he had landed on the deck itself, he might have survived, but his last vain attempt at taking hold of a rope to stop his fall caused his body to twist. The back of his neck struck the ship's port rail. He was instantly dead.

Shocked as he was at seeing this happen, Little Cock felt eyes on him and pulled his attention away from the confusion on the other ship to see Merit staring at him from the other ship's starboard rail. Bowing slightly from the waist, Merit smiled at Little Cock.

"Damn."

"Damn is right," said Captain KrommeZee. "And they say that *my* ship is cursed. Ha!" He grabbed hold of Little Cock's hand, the one that held Little Cock's gold coins, and none too gently pried open the fingers. He bit both coins, smiled at Little Cock, then pocketed them. "Two more like these and I would take you to the moon if you wished it."

KrommeZee looked past Little Cock, first to the commotion on the other ship, then at the docks, then over to the paths leading to the docks. "Where are your companions then?"

"On their way. There's something else." Little Cock indicated the barrel containing Jenny. "Is your vessel equipped with slave quarters?"

"Slave quarters! Amazing. An Indian with slaves. And a pirate to boot." He stepped back to look Little Cock over from head to toe and with a smile of respect. "Gold has great power, does it not?"

"Not me. No. I won't be going along on the voyage. I… Is there somewhere we can speak privately?"

The man with the scarred face had stopped what he was doing and was now staring with narrowed, thinking eyes at Little Cock.

"Follow me," said KrommeZee. "We'll go to my quarters."

Little Cock leaned down to the barrel to roll it.

"Leave that here for God's sake! No one will even think to steal your abominable whisky. We have plenty of rum on board. Don't we boys?"

From the center of the deck, out of the opening to the hold below, a scarfed head popped up. "Plenty of rum. From a pirate ship the rum has come just like me mum." The head disappeared with a crazy giggle.

"Yes," said Willem KrommeZee. "Indeed it did." And he walked aft toward the captain's quarters.

As Little Cock followed, he tried to pass by the man with the scarred face but the man stepped in front of him, blocking his way. "Do I know you?"

When Little Cock looked up, he saw that only one side of the man's face was scarred. Being back on a ship with a man he'd sailed three years with brought the man's name up from the depths of memory. "Bosselé! Bumpy! Is it really you?" Little Cock reached up to embrace the big man. "You remembered me."

"Not the name," said Bosselé engulfing Little Cock in an equally warm hug. "You lost your sister. Pretty girl she was. Very young to be set ashore in that place." He shook his head as he released him. "Ah. Your name was initials only. I remember that much."

Quietly: "I was known as L.C., but here I will be Pierce."

"Ah. Of course." Bosselé released him. "I don't blame you. L.C. was short for Lost Cause, right? Meaning you?" His laugh was as big as he was and just as compassionate.

KrommeZee turned. "Do you want to tell me something or not? And as for you, Terrence, I'll not have dawdling on my ship. Get back to work."

"Terrence?"

Bosselé shrugged, "Any port in a storm, hé, matey? I don't want anyone knowing my real name, either. I'll accept Terrence." Another quick hug and off he went to finish securing the last gun. "Pierce. Must be short for something obnoxiously Puritan. Or would that be Puritanly obnoxious? I'll figure it out. Good to see you, matey." He waved.

"Bosselé. One moment please." Bosselé stepped in, leaned down. Little Cock reached up to embrace his long-ago friend again and took the opportunity to whisper, "Keep an eye on that bâtard with the leather bag and the musket on the other ship. He's one of the reasons for our deception. And there's a live one in the barrel. Much more precious than any whisky. For my sake, guard it with your life."

Bosselé stepped back and although it seemed impossible that he could get any larger than he already was, he did. "That I promise, my friend. That I promise. I'm so sorry for what I did to her."

As Bosselé turned away, Little Cock thought he saw a glint of water in his eyes.

"Coming, Captain. I appreciate your time." Little Cock climbed the steps to the captain's quarters but before he opened to door to enter, something made him turn back.

Below him, the scarfed head had popped up again. "I wonder what's really in that barrel." Arms bulging with strength, the man propelled himself up onto the deck. From the knee down, his left leg was polished wood.

"Touch it and more than your leg will be woodpecker food, Woodpecker Food," said Bosselé barring the scarfed man's way.

Twelve

It was after the midday meal and I was in Monsieur St-Amand's personal quarters at the fort trying to pin up my hair in the mirror over his bureau. This was a new task I had learned from Marguerite but was still having problems with doing because my braids made my hair wavy and I wasn't used to seeing myself while attempting a task like tending to my hair, especially with the image doing the opposite to what I was telling my hands to do. I had finally succeeded and was adjusting my new bonnet when I heard a terrible racket coming from outside. I wasn't sure if the cries and noises were coming from within the fort's gates or from outside them.

But when Monsieur St-Amand—"Master" now—knocked on the door and said "Come quickly. They have Jenny," I grabbed my new munti and my clothing bag in one hand and followed him with my other hand on top of my bonnet which I hated already.

"They have Jenny? Who has Jenny?" It seemed that our adventure had begun and might be ending at the same time.

As we ran through the yard to the gate, I saw four soldiers wrestling one of our people toward the direction of the fort's jail.

It looked to be a difficult task for them as a fifth soldier showed up to assist. "How in God's name did he get out?"

From among them, a voice cried out "*Keskoua!*" It was Second Son.

And he was drunk and crying and fighting like an angry child who was overtired and hadn't gotten something he wanted. "Apal is gone. The baby needs to be fed."

"He picked the lock. We'll have to shackle him."

I stopped running. I needed to understand what Second Son had said. "Gone? What do you mean 'gone'?"

"Come on, you. Cooperate. We don't want to hurt you."

"But we will if we must."

"No. No. There she is. There's Keskoua. I must talk with her. My wife is dead. My son is hungry."

A loud *crack* at the gate made Monsieur St-Amand turn around to see where I was. He ran back and grabbed the wrist of the arm holding down my bonnet. "Someone is shooting his pistol," he said. "Hurry."

From behind us came a mournful wail with my name in it from Second Son. This reached into my stomach and made its way down into my belly where it grabbed there and threatened to expel itself in a gush of fear and sadness but I kept going. I called back, "Get someone to tell Rabbit Woman." Monsieur St-Amand pulled me along even faster. With the wind from my running speed I could feel my bonnet start to loosen. "Ce bonnet foutu!"

Monsieur St-Amand reached up and snatched the bonnet off my head and tucked it inside his jacket as we ran. With his jaw tight he said: "Let that foul word be the last French that comes out of your mouth until we arrive safely back at home."

"Which foul word? Bonnet?"

He didn't laugh.

"Who's shooting?" I didn't like the feel of this.

"For one thing, it appears that someone found Jacques l'Itale at the foot of The Bear. Head wound. Badly hurt but he's out there with Benny and Merit trying to take Jenny away. L'Itale says Hélène tried to kill him."

"Hélène? *My* Hélène? *My* Hélène tried to *kill somebody?*" I couldn't believe my ears. I stopped running again to learn that Monsieur St-Amand was much stronger than he looked. I could feel a sudden stretch of the shoulder of the arm he was dragging me along with. "*Ai.*"

"Come on!"

"Take it easy. I need that arm."

"Also, Little Cock is trying to get Jenny away from Jacques l'Itale and Merit."

"Good. That's good."

"No it isn't."

"App? Repeat?"

We reached the gate, which was a little more than half open. Monsieur St-Amand forced me behind it. "Stay there!" He snatched my munti and clothing bag from me, peered around the gate then started out into the open space where all the noise was coming from.

I grabbed the sleeve of his jacket. "What else is going on out there? I recognize my brother's voice."

"Benny's not engaged in any of the actual fighting. No surprise there. But he's waving pistols around like a mad fool and Gig is trying to stop him."

"Gig could get hurt! He's not used to pistols." I started out.

Monsieur St-Amand pushed me again back behind the gate. "I said. Stay there!" He pointed to where the gate's hinges connected it to the fort's outer wall. "You can watch through the jamb."

I took his advice. I could see that a tall muscled man with terrible scars along one side of his face and a wiry man with a wooden leg were trying—it looked to me—to take Jenteg from Merit and Jacques l'Itale. When Jacques l'Itale turned a certain way, allowing me to see the back of his head, it caused me concern for him. Hélène had done a job. It appeared that a piece of his skull was missing. I had to set my sympathies aside, though. This was serious business and the well-being of Jacques l'Itale was now the least of my worries. Most importantly, I didn't want Merit and Jacques l'Itale to have Jenteg any more than *she* did, yet it seemed to me that she didn't want the scarred man and the man with the wooden leg to have her either. She was kicking and punching out at all four men. Two soldiers appeared out of nowhere to help her but they weren't doing it very well. They were concentrating more on subduing Little Cock. I wasn't certain but it looked to me like Little Cock was trying to help the scarred man against the man with the wooden leg as well as trying to keep Merit and Jacques l'Itale away from Jenteg. One of the soldiers, the one I thought was trying to help Jenteg, was attempting to do this by pushing Little Cock out of the melee.

"*Stop!*" I yelled through the crack. "*Little Cock is helping her.*"

The soldiers at the fort had never liked or trusted Little Cock because he was always causing trouble even though he was vital to them for getting messages back and forth. They wouldn't be aware that he was on their side in this instance. I ran out from behind the gate and reached out to take hold of the soldier's shoulder to get his attention, to explain to him that Little Cock was a good fellow. I got myself an elbow in the breast for it. From behind me, Monsieur St-Amand threw his arm around my waist and dragged me away.

"Stay out of this, I said." He leaned down to pick up my munti and my bag and several other bags so I knew he was on the way to the ship with the supplies we'd stored in his quarters. "Stay out of this. We need you. We can't risk your getting injured." He ran off as well as he could with what looked to be about seven or eight bags in one hand. They must have been heavy as his other arm was up and far out to the side.

I glanced back to see that Gi'gwesu was struggling to hold Benny's left arm up in the air. That hand of Benny's held a pistol and I could see that its hammer had been pulled back. I looked down at Benny's right hand to see a pistol there, too. This one had smoke coming from it so I knew it was the one that had been fired. It would have to be reloaded and re-cocked. He let it fall to the ground before reaching around behind himself to draw yet another pistol from under his jacket. He pointed this one at Gi'gwesu just as Claude, Marguerite, and my daughter Jeanne came around the corner of the path. J-B was behind them with Claude and Marguerite's children following.

As soon as Marguerite noticed the fighting she turned to her children. "Allez. Allez. Go. Go. Allez chez nous. Go home."

J-B took immediate charge and spread his arms out to herd his brothers and sisters back along the path with Marguerite still urging them to go home.

Claude turned to Marguerite. "Surely to God they've seen enough drunken fights near the fort, ma chérie." This told me that Claude hadn't seen everything yet. He would soon need a pair of those spectacles that we had seen some Newcomers wearing.

Jeanne, then, was the first to see the pistol pointed at Gi'gwesu. She screamed and ran to leap onto Benny's back like a tqoqwej on an aplíkmuj, a lynx on a rabbit. She grabbed the arm with the pistol pointing at Gi'gwesu but this distraction only loosened Gi'gwesu's grip on Benny's left arm. Benny let that pistol fall and grabbed at the mechanism of the pistol in his right hand—the pistol that was pointing at Gi'gwesu's chest. I guessed that the mechanism was stuck or that Benny's thumb was not strong enough to pull the hammer back because he was having trouble with it. But then, even with Jeanne biting at him and scratching at his eyes and face from behind, he was able to cock it.

Marguerite screamed "*Stop him!*" and Claude leaped forward but not in time to stop the pistol from going off.

Gi'gwesu cried out and grabbed his side. "*Ah.*"

Benny now brought this pistol upward and behind him, attempting to strike the biting, scratching Jeanne with it and get her off his back. But before he could connect, she slipped to the ground and ran to help Gi'gwesu. Benny dropped the pistol.

The soldiers had turned instantly at the sound of Gi'gwesu's cry so abandoned Jenteg and Little Cock to help Claude subdue Benny who was in the process of bending to retrieve the still-cocked pistol that he'd let drop from his left hand. I hoped the powder had spilled out as it was quickly in Benny's left hand then in his right and was once more pointing at Gi'gwesu. But by now, Claude had gotten around behind Benny and had both arms part way around him, high up and wrapped around so Claude's hands were together behind Benny's neck. Benny's pistol made a circle in the air three times before it went off taking out a branch from a tall guow, a tall pine. From a neighboring guow, an atu'tuej chattered words much worse than the one I'd called my bonnet by. Claude had swung Benny around and away from Gi'gwesu so I could see Claude's face, his eyes. I knew that with one quick snap forward of Claude's clasped hands Benny would never be a problem to anyone again except those charged with transporting his dead body to a ship home. I think maybe the soldiers saw this in Claude's eyes, too. They quickly tore the pistol from Benny's hands. They were far from gentle about it.

The taller of the soldiers slid Claude's arms down off the back of Benny's neck. "Doucement, mon ami, Doucement. Easy, my friend. Easy. Bien joué. Well played."

The other soldier, the one I knew as Iggie, said to Benny. "Off to our jail with you, Maudit anglais." He twisted Benny's arm around behind. "You can't come in here firing your pistols at our people."

The other soldier stepped up to help Iggie restrain him.

Over to the side where Little Cock, the man with the half-scarred face and the man with the wooden leg had been struggling over Jenteg, with each other, and with Merit and Jacques l'Itale, it seemed that the battle was over. Jenny was now tucked safely in Little Cock's hug. I was surprised to see that the other two men were standing, feet apart and with fists ready in front of them.

Jacques l'Itale was still close to them but had turned his back to that group and was standing there, swaying slightly. His eyes seemed to be looking far away into the sky over the fort. I turned to look but there was nothing there, not even a bird. I'm not sure if Merit had moved away from Little Cock and his fellows because he knew he had been defeated, or if he really believed he could stop the soldiers from taking Benny in as a roommate for Second Son in the fort's jail. He stepped forward, but paused for a moment because four more soldiers had arrived to assist. I recognized them as the ones who had been wrestling with Second Son earlier. Second Son would be safe from self-harm. At least for the moment. I only hoped that someone had sent for Rabbit Woman so she could tend to Apal's baby. And what would most likely be Apal's dead body. I felt sadness moving up from inside of me but knew I didn't have time right now to be sad or worried. We had to get away.

"I say!" Benny struggled to get the hands of the soldiers off him.

Merit puffed himself up, moved in: "Get your hands off him. Immediately."

Jacques l'Itale, his eyes like slits, staggered up to stand beside Merit and in a drunken voice agreed. "Yes. You've no place to right manner. Never at all."

No. Jacques l'Itale was not drunk. The blow to his head had been a hard one. He was suffering from it. His words made no sense.

Iggie said: "You, too, l'Itale. Come with us."

Yet another set of soldiers arrived and these were waving muskets around. "Go quietly," one of them ordered. "Take them away." All three of the New England men went along with the soldiers obediently, Benny brushing off invisible dust from his arms and chest. He walked straight with chin high to follow the lead man into the fort. Merit shrugged off the guiding hand of the soldier to his left. Jacques l'Itale went along like a child going with his mother into a new part of a forest.

The man who had ordered the soldiers to take the New England men away came to me and said quietly. "We've sent someone to alert Rabbit Woman that the drunk fellow's wife and son need tending to. Just thought you'd like to know." He stood there looking at me with a question in his eyes.

"Thank you," I said. "Merci."

He smiled but made no effort to stop looking at me.

"Merci. Merci *beaucoup*. Thank you a lot. But excuse me, I must tend to my brother." I moved away but I could still feel his questions at my back. He had recognized me but could not place who I was with my hair like this and my New England clothing.

Monsieur St-Amand had already raised Gig's shirt and was examining his wound. "It appears that the shot clipped a rib. Cracked it but the only danger will be infection as it didn't enter the body." He turned to me. "Rabbit Woman has the knowledge of treating infections and wounds like this?"

I nodded.

"What do you mean, Rabbit Woman?" demanded Gi'gwesu loudly then gasped. "*Aii!*" He grabbed at his side and on touching his wound gasped again. "I'm going with you. I promised. Jenny needs me."

"You are not going anywhere," I said. "I'll make sure nothing happens to her."

"I can't put that on you. *Aii.*" He spoke more quietly: "I promised her. And you... were only going... because of me."

"That's right," said my daughter, Jeanne, taking my hand to hold it between hers. "You don't have to go now."

"That's why people should never make promises. Things happen.

And yes, I do have to go."

Jeanne threw her arms around me and squeezed me hard. "Please don't go, Mama. It's too dangerous. Gig needs you. We all need you."

I removed her arms from around me and cupped her face in my hands. "Yes. It is dangerous. You see it. You see the need for us to go and rescue Jenteg's daughter and… uh…" The scarred man and the man with the wooden leg were peering over at us. I hoped they hadn't heard us. "We also need to rescue a certain person's sister. From people like these." I tilted my head toward the scarred man and the man with the wooden leg.

The man with the wooden leg huffed. The other man grinned.

"But—"

"Do you not understand the need?"

Monsieur St-Amand stepped over to the scarred man and the man with the wooden leg and spoke quietly with them. The scarred man took the arm of the man with the wooden leg and guided him away. Monsieur St-Amand indicated that Little Cock should go with them.

I kissed Jeanne's forehead. "Have you not learned that if you have the talent—the ability—to do something when there are no others capable, that it is *your* responsibility?" I let her face go and turned to Monsieur St-Amand who pointed with his thumb in the direction of the ship. His face told me our time was running out. "Look after your uncle Gig for me, will you?"

"Na t'oq, Giju'. Na t'oq. I love you."

"I love you, tutji'j. And I want you to help look after Tities, Su'n and Nalagit, too. That should keep you busy enough to take your mind off your worries, e'e?"

"E'e."

I then went over to Jenteg. "You all right, Jenny?"

She adjusted her clothing and nodded. "Just keep these two away from me."

Little Cock, who had been speaking quietly to the scarred man, returned to take her elbow. "You sure you are all right?"

She shrugged away. "What were you doing helping them?"

"I was helping you." He put his hand on his back and stretched to one side. "You have a powerful kick there, girl."

"Oh, did I get you? I'm sorry. I…"

"You're forgiven. Let's go. Oh. Please meet two of the crew." He motioned them over. "Bosselé, also called Terrence." Little Cock giggled at this, *Terrence* did not. "And this is?"

"He's called Woodpecker Food," said Bosselé. "And if any trouble ever starts up, he is most likely at the heart of it." With this, he gave Woodpecker Food such a hard pat on the back it made him stagger. "Whether on board a ship or in a tavern, right, Woody?"

Woodpecker Food grunted.

"Too curious, this one. Too curious."

"We must board the ship *now*," said Monsieur St-Amand, indicating the several soldiers that were coming back out from the fort. "Gig will be fine." He turned to Little Cock. "Pierce?"

"Yes, Master," said Little Cock, his smile wide.

"You're coming with us. Help the ladies along. I mean the girls. We have run out of time. They're already raising the sails."

"Yes, Master."

I was equally worried and happy that Little Cock was coming with us.

Thirteen

I wasn't prepared for the hundreds of ropes all over the ship. They were everywhere and each of them was attached to something at both ends. The bottom ends were coiled into neat round piles. As I looked around at them all, I thought I might now understand what a bug sees when it's inside a spider's web. I hoped I wouldn't get caught in any of them. Little Cock had taught us a lot of terms about ships and crews and captains but I had a feeling I was going to be learning a lot more of them during our journey to the port of Boston. I was happy about this, I always liked learning new words and languages. I liked the ship. It was new so didn't yet have that strong, strong smell of sea on it. Sorry, on *her*. "Ships are always she," Little Cock had told us. I wondered if maybe this was the real reason *she* didn't like to have women on board. Maybe it had nothing to do with bringing storms at all, but because ships were jealous of other females. I went below.

It didn't take long for me to get the story out of Jenny as to why she ended up in the yard in front of the fort fighting off four men. While she was helping me put away my things in "Master Gooden's" cabin, she told me.

She had been in the whisky barrel on deck so could hear everything going on.

"One voice said: 'I wonder what's really in that barrel.' Another replied: 'Touch it and more than your leg will be woodpecker food.'"

"So this man with the wooden leg…?"

"He opened my barrel. I was grateful for the fresh air. He looked in at me. I saw the surprise on his face. Which I could accept. But then came a certain smile which I could not accept. He began to lift me out. I think out of some measure of kindness mixed in with the lust, now that I think back on it. But initially, all I could see was the lust. I began to cry out, hoping the other man, the one who had threatened him, would hear me and save me from this one. I can't even hide in a whisky barrel without men causing me problems."

I laughed at this and got a click of tongue for it so put my smile away. "So he? He did what? Pull you out and try to carry you away with him?"

"No, not at all." She folded the last of my underskirts and tucked them into the bottom drawer of the ornate bureau in Master Gooden's cabin while I put the clothing bag and my munti onto a shelf behind an elaborately paneled narrow door in the wall of the cabin. In the mirror above the bureau, I checked my hair and adjusted my bonnet around it. Nothing was hanging out. I was pleased about that. And surprised too.

We closed the door to the cabin and started along the passageway.

"It wasn't he who caused the problem. In retrospect, he was being kind," she said when we reached the ladder to below. "Even so, I would not trust being alone with him anywhere." Her eyes sent me the message that I should be careful around this man, too.

She handed her bags to me and started down first. When she reached the bottom, I lowered her bags to her with their long shoulder straps then started down myself. It wasn't easy in my bulky skirts, underskirts, restricting bodice and undergarments.

She said: "In my experience, most men carry their brains in their nether parts."

I almost lost my grip on the ladder with the sudden laugh that burst from me.

We were two decks below the main deck now. We expected the worst because the walls—oh, sorry, the bulkheads—stretched from one end of the ship to the other leaving only a narrow passageway. They were plain smoothed wood from what I could see; they still smelled of the oak they were made from; and five simple doors had been cut into them. I didn't want to see what might be behind those doors.

A piece of paper was nailed to the nearest door:

Pierce & Jenny

"Ah," Jenny said. "A lovely welcome note. Perhaps a harbinger of better things to come?" Her face held no sign of hope. "I've seen the insides of cargo rooms before. At least it looks like there will be only two of us in the stinking hold. I'm glad it's a new ship."

But when Jenny lifted the latch, I think both of our chins must have dropped at the same time because when we looked at each other, her mouth was as wide open as I knew mine was. The cabin that Little Cock and Jenteg would be staying in was clean and spacious with double wooden cots, one on top of the other, and with not one but two windows over highly polished table desks with storage shelves beneath them, one set of shelves already filled with clothing and other items. Little Cock had already unpacked.

"You have two windows," I said. "We have one."

"And we have two beds. Where you have only the one."

I hadn't thought about that. Hadn't even noticed as I was overcome by all the fancy decorations on the walls of Monsieur St-Amand's cabin and the thickly upholstered furniture and velvet curtains held back with ribbons.

"You won't be cold at night."

I detected a bitterness in her words that was the furthest thing from jealousy imaginable.

"Do you trust him?" she asked.

"Do I have a choice?"

"He seems like an honorable man. There are choices and there are choices. The chair in his room is large and looks like it would be quite comfortable. Perhaps he will prove to be more gentleman than any of us expect from a man, yes?"

"I'm almost sure of it, yes."

"You can be honorable as well and take turns in the chair. Yes?"

"Yes." I hoped the journey before us would not be long enough to stir feelings beyond those we already had for each other. I loved Falcon, my husband, but a month—maybe even more—was a long time away from love.

"From what I have seen of him, what I feel of him, I too believe he is not the sort of man to force himself on a woman. I am certain of that. Especially on you." She turned her back fully to me and pretended to busy herself with something while she asked: "You know he's in love with you, don't you?"

This was something I didn't want to put into my head so I changed the subject. "So. How do you like your 'slave quarters,' Jenny?"

It seemed to me that a whole thundercloud of cares came out of Jenteg from somewhere deep down inside her. Arms wide, she raised her face to the ceiling and spun around twice before tossing her bags onto the bottom cot. "It is not nearly as terrible here as I thought it would be. And look!" She reached up to grasp the edge of a curtain tucked into a space in the wall between the windows. She pulled it out and its metal hoops whispered along a long rod that went all the way to the edge of the entrance door, dividing the room into two equal sections. She slid it back and tucked it away. "A modesty curtain. How thoughtful." She seemed at peace for the first time since coming into our lives. "You didn't answer my question."

"And I don't intend to." I started to fold her clothes as she had helped me fold mine. "So what really happened?"

"Merit happened."

"Merit?"

"A man with a leather bag. One so strongly muscled he could split his shirt without trying?"

"That's the one, yes."

"He was on the deck of that next ship." She turned her head one way then the other, then pointed in the direction of the bow. "The one that way. He saw me come out of the barrel."

"Why was he on that other ship, I wonder. Oh, wait." I sucked in my breath. "They found out you were hiding at Hélène's and they were ready to set sail immediately once they had you."

"Yes. They sent Jacques l'Itale up there to get me. That didn't work out very well for Jacques l'Itale."

"They were going to take you away on that other ship."

"Yes."

"That's better than what I heard they were going to do to y— Oh!" Once again my thought came out of my mouth too quickly.

"What did you say?"

"Never mind. I heard something. One of their plans. But it all worked out, didn't it?"

Jenteg's eyes narrowed at me but she didn't ask the question that must have been in her head. Maybe she knew the answer already. "The next thing I knew, he and l'Itale—he looks a fright, doesn't he?—came on board and took me. Benny was waiting on the dock, all smiles."

Jenteg's meager belongings were now stored away on the shelves under the right hand desk. Her bag went into a closet similar to the one in Master Gooden's cabin. It was not quite as highly decorated, but still beautiful.

"When they were dragging me down the gangplank, the man called Woodpecker Food came running after them calling out 'Leave her be. She's mine. I found her so she's mine. Stop, thieves. Thieves.' He even fired a shot at them. I guess this alerted what's his name? Bossy something?"

"Bosselé."

"Bosselé. Yes. Well, he came off the ship yelling like a mad man and it seemed to me trying to stop Woodpecker Food from stopping those men. I suppose Bosselé didn't know who they were. They began acting like they were trying to save me from Woodpecker Food. The liars! I didn't know what to think so I just fought against all of them as best I could."

"You did well. You got off a nice shot to Little Cock's kidney. What was it? Your foot?"

"I don't think he was too badly hurt by it. Just looking for compassion from me. Did he want me to kiss it better?" I liked her laugh. "But oh, I feel sorry for Jacques l'Itale even though I have nothing but contempt for him and his fellows. I don't like to see anybody in that condition. He was trying to help his fellows but every time he tried to strike out, he missed. He fell twice that I recall. And at one point seemed to forget whose side he was on."

"What happened to him? I saw the back of his head." I didn't have much of a care for Jacques l'Itale either but he was still a person and things didn't look good for him. An infection in the brain would be a bad thing and not just for him. When people had brain injuries and infections in their brains they sometimes had violent fits and didn't know who was who. It could be dangerous for everybody.

"Hélène happened to him. Well, her frying pan happened to him when I was hiding outside their house. Hiding in the trees with J-B. The frying pan was full of meat and eggs, she said." Jenteg leaned over with her hands on her knees while a laugh burst from her. "Worth a lost breakfast, she said. I shouldn't laugh but I can't help it. She was so proud of herself."

"François took l'Itale up to The Bear so people would think he fell. You know, instead of getting Hélène in trouble. He's very good to her, isn't he?"

"Yes, he is. So, he just left Jacques there?"

"He said he was going to set things up to make it look like—" Her laughter was getting stronger. She could barely talk anymore. "Somebody must have found him. Or else he came to and found himself."

"His injury is really serious. From what I could see."

She was still laughing so hard she could only nod. I think she had the same problem as Little Cock. Hers from never having been happy, his from never knowing that he could be. I began to be concerned that her laughter might turn into something else, like a crying fit, when from above, loud voices came down to us.

"Something's going on up there." I grabbed her elbow. "Let's go see."

She recovered herself from her laughing. "That felt good."

"I'm sure it did." It made me feel good, too, to see her laugh.

***

At the top of the ladder to the main deck, I stuck my head up to see many men scurrying here and there. At first it looked like total confusion with Captain yelling orders and Bosselé yelling orders and some men going up the rigging and others coming down. Ropes were everywhere but organized and controlled. Marguerite had taught me how to weave on a loom so for me to see how these men were able to put so many ropes together and have it come out so perfectly made me feel less afraid about what might be ahead of us. These men knew what they were doing. And they were doing it fast.

Bosselé came over to help me up then reached down for Jenteg who was right below me on the ladder. "Normally, we don't allow the inexperienced on deck at a time like this, but this frenzy seems to be in your honor, Miss Jenny." He pointed. "See the aft cannon starboard, ladies?"

"You mean that one?" I asked.

"Stand there. Stay standing there. And be aware that men on shore have fired at us already."

We rushed to the rail to see what was happening.

Benny was waving a pistol in each hand. Merit had somehow gotten hold of two muskets. One was lying on the ground behind him and it appeared he was checking the load on the other. A soldier lay on the ground at his feet. The soldier stirred so I knew he was alive. It was Iggie. Another soldier came to help him up. Then Iggie and the soldier who had helped him grabbed hold of Merit to pry the musket from his hands but they couldn't. Merit was a strong man.

Claude stepped in front of Benny and I called down to him. "Look out, Claude. He has pistols."

Claude cupped his hands around his mouth and called out. "The damned lapointes let these bâtards go. They wouldn't listen to me. No."

"He has *pistols.* Look out!"

"Pas de problème, chérie. At least the maudits lapointes took their powder and shot. And look over there."

I looked where Claude had told me to see that the ship beside us was slowly pulling away from the dock and was now the length of a snawe'l, a sugar tree, away from it. Down below it on the dock, Jacques l'Itale was shaking his fist and calling the men on board that ship names that were both familiar and unfamiliar. A man I guessed was the Captain called down. "I told you people the ship is not ready to sail. The repairs are not finished."

Jacques l'Itale said something that told me he didn't believe the Captain.

"Besides, I will not set sail on a Friday. Go away. Come back tomorrow." The Captain turned away to give orders to the men on his ship.

Without any sign that something might be wrong, Jacques l'Itale fell sideways onto the dock below. At first I thought he might have been shot but I hadn't heard that now-familiar *crack*. He rose to his feet and looking confused, turned toward our ship. He blinked several times then started for our gangplank.

Benny had obviously heard what the Captain of the other ship had called out to Jacques l'Itale because Benny walked as fast as he could to our gangplank, too. His face got redder and redder the closer he came. Merit, now on the ground with no fewer than five soldiers wrestling with him, yelled: "All right. All right. Take the goddamn thing. Let me up. I have to go with my boss."

Iggie retrieved his musket from the pile of Merit and soldiers, dumped the powder out of it, then raced to and up our gangplank. Jacques l'Itale and Benny were half way to it. At the top of our gangplank, Iggie reached into the pouch at his hip to bring out what I knew would be powder and shot. He loaded in the time it would take to breathe once. He cocked it. Raised it. I had never seen him so angry. "Back off. *Merde à Dieu, vous fils de pute. J'vais vous tuer. Dégagez.* I'll shoot, I tell you. I'll damned well shoot. Get off that gangplank *immédiatement*, immediately!"

This stream of words I'd rarely heard, even from Claude's mouth, did nothing to frighten Benny and Jacques l'Itale. They started up the gangplank.

"Get back, I say. Maudit!"

Captain KrommeZee hurried to the rail. "What in the name of—?" He took a quick look at what was going on then called out. "Cast off all lines from the bollards!"

Below, two dock hands uncoiled ropes from around two mooring posts while several men on our ship pulled the ropes in with long movements of their arms. Behind me, Woodpecker Food called out from the ship's wheel. "Ready at the helm, Sir."

Captain KrommeZee then spoke quietly to Iggie. "There will be no deaths on this ship while I'm captain of it. Belay that musket, sir."

Iggie did not change position.

Captain KrommeZee made a head motion to the three crew who stood to his right. He said something I couldn't hear.

As one, the men smiled wide and said "Yes, Sir, Captain Sir." Two more crew who had been standing close, joined them at the top of the gangplank. Laughing, each man went about his task.

A medium-tall man with a bald head said "Grab hold" and he and a second man took hold of the left-hand ropes of the gangplank. On the other side of Iggie, who still pointed his musket at Benny and Jacques l'Itale, the other two men did the same.

The man I would soon know as Tommy had taken a long pole into his hands and reached over the rail to push against the dock with it. At first, nothing happened, but when he put his weight into it again, muscles bulging, I could see that the dock was moving slightly away from us. Well, more correctly, we were moving away from the dock. A loud scream of wood on wood told me the gangplank was scraping across the dock. It was now only a blue jay's wing from the edge.

Bosselé appeared at my side. He was holding a roll of what looked like rigging with two hooks. "Usually the Captain orders the gangplank raised *before* cast off. This'll be good."

I then understood what was about to happen and I couldn't help myself. I laughed out loud.

Benny looked up at me. Down at his feet. Up at Captain KrommeZee. Then behind him where Jacques l'Itale stood, face blank once more, mouth slightly open. Benny turned, pushed Jacques l'Itale aside against the rope handrail, then scampered as best he could to the dock end of the gangplank. Tommy gave another enormous push with his pole and off from the dock went the end of the gangplank just as Benny reached the dock with his leading foot. He might have been able to control men with his authority but he was not as fortunate with commanding his body to obey. His rear foot stayed where it was on the gangplank so pulled him backwards. He fell against Jacques l'Itale knocking him down. Both men slid into the water between the ship and the dock. The gangplank banged against the hull of our ship. Iggie lowered his musket and stepped away, releasing its hammer as he did so. I could now see his face. He was trying to be serious like a lapointe is supposed to, but he wasn't doing a very good job of it. The smile was coming out of his eyes. The four crew hauled the gangplank up by its ropes and slid it against the rail where they secured it with—yes—more ropes. Bosselé tossed the roll of rigging to Claude who was standing below; Claude caught it then hooked it onto the dock's edge and let it roll down to the water. It was a ladder.

"Hé, Maudit anglais. Climb to Heaven on this."

The lapointes holding Merit had let him go by this time and he rushed to help Benny get over the ledge at the top of the ladder. He left Jacques l'Itale to his own devices.

Claude put a hand down to help Jacques l'Itale up and over. A dock hand assisted. Both were looking down at the top of Jacques l'Itale's head as they did this. The dock hand frowned. Claude looked up at me and with his free hand, pointed at Jacques l'Itale's head and made much the same face as the dock hand had. Claude reached down and hesitated twice before he reached into the hole in Jacques l'Itale's head to pluck a piece of what I thought was probably seaweed out of it. This did not look good for Jacques l'Itale. The salt water would kill some microbes. But not all of them. I feared for his life.

Merit had removed his jacket and had wrapped it across Benny's shoulders. He was leading him away.

"What shall we do with this one?" Claude shouted up to me and Monsieur St-Amand, who was now standing beside me clucking his tongue.

"Take him to Rabbit Woman," Monsieur St-Amand and I said at exactly the same time. We laughed although we knew nothing was funny.

Beside us, Bosselé spoke. "Best go below to your quarters for a while. We are underway so you will be underfoot." To Iggie he said. "Looks like you're stuck with us, soldier. Come with me, I'll show you where you will be sleeping for the next few weeks or so." Bosselé stood back and looked Iggie up and down. "You look about the same size as Lars. Perhaps if you treat him well, he'll lend you something more seaworthy than what you're wearing."

"Bring him to my quarters when he's done," said Monsieur St-Amand. "I want to know why they released those men from the fort."

***

As we moved farther and farther away from shore, the clouds parted for a moment and I could see that Moon, almost full, was already climbing. Sun was saying goodbye from the other side of the sky, his light visible as a thin line. Like the curtains in Jenteg's cabin, the clouds closed over Moon's face again to give her privacy until it was her time to fill the sky with her own light. I looked back to see Benny and Jacques l'Itale shivering on the dock, both wrapped so tightly in blankets, they looked like sleeping caterpillars. There would be no beautiful butterflies coming out of these cocoons, though. Benny took a moment to remove one arm from inside his wrap to shake his fist at us. He hollered some words that were swallowed up by the loud voices of men behind me calling out orders about adjusting the topsail. On shore, over to the right, I spotted Merit with a handful of a fat fellow's shirt front as he pointed with the other hand to a small boat with its hind end bobbing up and down in the lapping waves, no longer glistening with Sun's last light of the day. Several men—I assumed they were this fellow's booty mates—were closing in, sticks and poles in their hands. Merit released the man's shirt and stepped away just as Sun took the last bit of light along with him to put what happened next behind a curtain of shadows. I heard no cries, no shouts of anger, so knew that Merit had made the right decision and would go unharmed.

When the clouds moved away from Moon's face again, Captain KrommeZee came up to stand with us. "Perfect sailing weather, Edward my friend." His long arm reached over Monsieur St-Amand's back to embrace him. "Waxing moon, quiet sea, good winds, receding tide in the direction we want to go—and all our troubles left ashore, yes?"

"I hope so, Willem" said Monsieur St-Amand. "I pray so."

"Don't tell me you are superstitious, too," said Captain KrommeZee. "I thought you surgeon-types knew better."

Monsieur St-Amand didn't return Captain KrommeZee's enthusiastic smile. "If you want my input, I think a name on her would draw less attention. A lot less. And word will get out fast—name on her or not—that she has not been christened."

"I hate to be the one to inform you," said Captain KrommeZee with disdain, "religious *baptisms* are no longer in fashion. Groundless fears, I say. And I've not come up with a name for her yet because I don't want to name her after my wife but feel I must. Yet my wife insists I name it after her mother, which I absolutely do not want to do. A conundrum, yes? Perhaps I'll just sink her when I get into deep water to keep the peace and save my neck."

He laughed at this but in a way that made me wonder if he really meant to do it.

Fourteen

Jenteg had suggested—with winks and smiles—that Monsieur St-Amand and I would be spending much of our time alone in his cabin. I think even if Monsieur St-Amand and I had wanted to be alone, we would have had trouble arranging it because, for the next several days, there was a steady stream of visitors to *our* cabin, most of them the very first morning.

We were enjoying our break-fast meal, Captain KrommeZee and Monsieur St-Amand eating at a drop-down table against the wall farthest from me while I ate cross-legged on the bed. Sun's light flowed in through the single window to make the panels on the bulkhead opposite appear to be on fire. I didn't know that wood could be so beautiful when it was carved, stained and polished like that. A young man of about fifteen winters had delivered the food to us. Captain had referred to him as the cabin boy.

But before this young man arrived, all solicitous and bowing and smiling at Monsieur St-Amand, Captain had told me, much to my surprise, "I know who you really are so I would very much enjoy your company at table with us, but you understand that most of the crew—with very few exceptions—believe you to be Dawn the slave owned by Edward Gooden. You'll have to sit there."

I lowered my rear end to the bed.

He continued. "And although the cabin boy is answerable to me, as are you, that does not make you equal in the eyes of the law to him. Do you understand?"

I tried not to roll my eyes but I don't think I managed very well.

"And none of that," said Monsieur St-Amand. "You'll get us all killed."

"Na t— Hmm! Yes, Master." My gaze sought a spot on the floor.

Carrying a large tray filled with dishes and bowls and mugs, Cabin Boy entered. With the grace of a dancer, he removed everything from the tray and placed it on the table. I was invisible. He stepped out quietly but before he could close the door behind him, Little Cock, cap in hand, entered.

"You summoned me, Master." Head down, he twisted his cap around in his fingers.

"Stop doing that with your cap!"

"Master?"

"Willem here is fully aware of our entire plan. Relax."

"Yes, Mas—"

Captain KrommeZee spoke. "I know you only as Pierce and that's the best way to have it." He lifted the lid from a pot and began to spoon out what looked like broken up hard-cooked eggs mixed with some kind of meat onto a plate. "I told Edward here that last night you were overacting your part as slave. We thought it best to warn you of the dangers of doing that." From a large, clear glass bowl, he took out an apple. From under a silver cover, a small roll of bread. He placed what I knew was a knife and spoon rolled into a napkin on the side of the plate. "For Dawn. Would you be so kind?" He held out the plate to Little Cock who handed it over to me. "Thank you." He turned to Monsieur St-Amand. "Shall I continue? Or?"

With a mouthful of food, Monsieur St-Amand motioned with his knife that Captain KrommeZee should continue.

"Have you eaten, Pierce?"

"I have, Sir. Thank you."

"I understand the need to be seen as inferior and servile to your master here. It's important that we all play our parts in this business, much of which you are not yet a party to. However. May I speak bluntly?"

Little Cock nodded. He had stuffed his cap into a back pocket of his pants.

"I'm afraid that you and Dawn here." He smiled at me with kindness. "Are at opposite ends of what might be expected behavior for a slave. You, Pierce, are much, much too obsequious in your mannerisms around me and the crew and especially Edward here. And our Miss Dawn is not nearly respectful enough." One eyebrow went up at me.

I knew that was coming.

"I suggest you put your heads together. Include Jenny in your discussions. She has an exceptional amount of personal experience with these matters. Need I continue?" From under his eyebrows, his eyes traveled back and forth between Little Cock and me.

I nodded agreement.

"Advice accepted," said Little Cock and he turned to leave.

"One more thing, Pierce."

Little Cock turned back.

"Some of the crew have shown what I will refer to as an *interest* in Dawn. Especially one called Gregor. Do you understand what I mean by that? They do see her as a slave, you know. Fair game as it were." He shook his head. "Pigs."

Monsieur St-Amand set down his knife and spoon and dabbed his lips with his napkin. He tucked what he had been chewing over to one side of his mouth. "Why wasn't I informed of this?"

"I thought you knew. It *is* rather obvious."

"I did not know." He turned to me. "If any one of those men lays so much as a finger on you, I expect you to inform me instant—"

"If you'd wait for just a moment, Edward, I'll explain my intentions."

"And what might those intentions be, Willem? Do you plan to throw your whole crew to the sharks?"

"If need be."

Little Cock blinked. Monsieur St-Amand's mouth popped open showing me the piece of gristle he had been so politely attempting to work into swallowing consistency. And I said, "Really! To protect me you would endanger us all by tossing everyone who knows anything about getting this boat of yours—"

"Ship. It's a ship," Little Cock whispered loudly at me out of the side of his mouth. "Not a boat. Never a boat to a captain! I told you that."

"Sorry, Sir. Ship! Getting this *ship* of yours back onto solid ground?"

"Terrence and Woody—Bosselé and Woodpecker Food as you know them—have been watching out for you from before we launched and they have orders to continue doing so." He turned to Little Cock. "And they have been assigned to watch out for you as well."

Little Cock and I asked the same question together: "And Jenny? What about Jenny?"

"Especially Jenny. Unfortunately, she can't remain in her cabin for the whole voyage. She will need fresh air and daily exercise on the main deck. We will have to keep her face and body veiled."

"Like the Arabs do," laughed Little Cock. "To keep marauders from stealing the pretty ones and leaving the ugly ones behind."

I couldn't help myself. That was really funny to hear.

"I heard that story, too." Captain KrommeZee laughed along with me. "But I take little store in it. Although it does give a more plausible reason than blaming everything on lustful angels. What say you, Edward? Which side do you take in this?"

"I say, cover Jenny by all means and hope the angels story is true. I think our crew—several of whom are Arabs judging by the color of their skin, their narrow noses, their noble demeanor and obvious intelligence—might think along the former lines and decide she must be even more beautiful than Kes— even more beautiful than my Dawn." He smiled over at me.

"Why not veil her, too, then?" suggested Little Cock, tipping his head toward me. "Anything to keep her safe."

I knew his idea was coming from his concern for me but I didn't want that. "I'm restricted enough having to wear this regalia." I grabbed my skirt with both hands and spread it wide to demonstrate. "Try wearing all this from morning till night. I'd sink like a bag of crab bait if I fell off the boa— ship."

"We all three will keep an eye out," said Captain KrommeZee, placing his napkin on the table beside his plate and rising from his chair. "Bosselé is more than determined to keep you safe. He knows how important you are to Edward." He adjusted his belt and buttoned his jacket over his stomach. "I'll take my coffee at the helm this morning. I'll send my cabin boy in with yours. I understand you have a meeting? So. Three mugs then. Shall we join each other again for lunch, Edward? My cabin?"

Monsieur St-Amand raised his eyebrows at me.

I nodded.

"Of course, Willem. We have much to discuss."

Captain KrommeZee brought his huge hand down onto Little Cock's back. "You are lucky to have such loyal friends. Especially in Bosselé. Right, Pierce?"

"Right," said Little Cock. "He knows for certain where my sister is. He told me last night."

"That's wonderful, Little Cock. You've almost found her," I said too loudly as I rushed over to hug him. Although ships' walls—bulkheads—

were made of wood, voices traveled through them just as easily as they did through wikuom walls. In a normal voice, I told him. "See? You took your first step and now you are able to see that things *can* fit together sometimes. I am so happy for you. Your sister is alive and well. Where is she?"

Little Cock lowered his head. "Bosselé refused to tell me. All he would say was 'In due time you'll know.' I don't like the sound of that. Not at all."

***

No sooner had Cabin Boy put everything back onto his huge silver tray to carry it away and Captain KrommeZee and Little Cock had left, than Iggie came knocking. From what I had seen so far—although it had been less than a day—Iggie wasn't displeased with having been accidentally trapped on board when the crew let the gangplank fall with Benny and Jacques l'Itale still on it. Iggie was already helping several of the crew with chores. I had a feeling he might decide to change his life from soldier to sailor. Or that perhaps he had changed from sailor to soldier and now back again? There was more to Iggie than I had ever thought there might be.

"Here I am." He looked comfortable in his borrowed clothes. "At your service." He made a deep bow with a long sweeping motion of his right hand as though he held a fancy feathered man's hat in it. I had seen Claude doing this when acting out stories for his children.

"Have a seat, Iggie. What can you—? Wait."

Cabin Boy drifted into the room then out again like smoke in a slow breeze, leaving behind three mugs, a bowl of what I recognized as New England sugar—even with the molasses out of it, cane sugar was pinker than maple sugar—spoons, and a pot of something hot. I had kept my own mug of tea. It was cool now, but I was used to drinking it like that.

And also, when Little Cock was teaching us about ships and the sea, he told us never to drink water that had not been boiled, and even then to be careful of it. "That's why we sailors trust only rum." I think that was supposed to be a joke but none of us laughed. Especially Little Cock.

Monsieur St-Amand made a motion with his head to Iggie that he should check the door. Then he held up one of the mugs and stretched that arm out to me. In his Master voice he asked: "Would you care to try a taste of coffee, Dawn?"

I played along. "Coffee, Master? Me?" I'd heard of it but hadn't tried it, not even when visiting with Claude and Marguerite who drank it every Sunday after Mass and at Christmas and Easter and on other occasions when there were visitors in their home other than relatives.

Iggie rose quietly, stepped to the door, pulled it open fast. I heard quick footsteps fading as Cabin Boy hurried away.

"You'll no doubt want it with sugar for your first taste of it. Shall I?" He held a spoon piled high with sugar over the mug he had offered.

"Coffee tastes good. And it's good *for* you," said Iggie as he sat back down. "In Paris, the literati have embraced it so strongly that now my parents keep it at home as a staple. Mother told the staff to keep it on the shelf beside the tea. Can you imagine! We drink it often, especially when visitors come."

So, I thought, *Marguerite is up to the times for not only New England fashions but for the latest practices in France as well.* It surprised me that it took so long for people to travel from place to place on their ships but the knowledge of new things flew ahead of them like seabirds. Or perhaps like sharks in some cases. Our people relied on our dreams to learn new ways of doing things. Most Newcomers thought we were all elue'wiet, crazy, for doing that. They prayed and told us that their god caused most things to happen but I had heard from Marguerite's cousin, Damoiselle Autoritaire (Charlotte), that the New Englanders believed that God controlled everything, that if you were born poor, that's the way God wanted you to stay. I found that hard to believe. What good was hope then? Why pray in the first place?

"My brother, my dear black sheep older brother and heir to the family fortune, once invited me to go to Paris's Café de Procope with him for coffee in the hopes of perhaps meeting royal figures. Or at least *someone* important." Iggie shrugged then took a sip from his own mug then set it back on the table. "But unfortunately, I was called to duty in Acadia. Perhaps when I go back to France, hé, Hermel?"

"Shh. Edward. You must call me Edward."

"Merde. J'ai oublié."

"And no French. You forgot that too? This is no time, or place, to be defiant."

Is Iggie in on our plans to rescue Jenteg's daughter and find Little Cock's sister?

Monsieur St-Amand interrupted my wondering by raising the mug to me again and gesturing at me with it. "Well? Feeling adventurous? This will be our last taste of it. Many Puritans look with suspicion upon those who drink other than tea. Coffee comes from the Arabs, the Muslim world, you see."

I didn't see. From what I knew, the Muslims and the Catholics and the Protestants—Puritan or not—all believed in the same god. Even Hélène's kind old friend who had taught her so much about life, the man they called Lesui'p, the Jew, prayed to the same one. I was always, and still am, confused that most Newcomers—both the French and the English—spoke of Jesus as being the most wonderful, loving, compassionate person who ever walked on Mother Earth and the Fathers told us constantly that people must be like Jesus and love everybody equally if they wanted to be happy—I think the Puritans said the same—but most people never even tried to be anything other than what they had always been: haters of each other. Maybe the Puritan view of Stay The Same was right?

"As far as most of those Puritan devils are concerned, Arabs are the devils." Iggie closed one eye at me. "Almost every bit of culture and higher ideas we have in the whole of Europe came from the Arabs but they are devils?" He raised his arms high and wide. "I don't understand people sometimes."

I was beginning to like Iggie.

He grasped his mug, raised it and took another sip of coffee. "Hmm. Excellent. Try it, Dawn. You'll like it."

I tried it. I did like it. Especially the sweetness of it but I wondered how it would taste without the big spoonful of cane sugar that Monsieur St-Amand had put in it. Cane sugar had a different taste from what I was used to. I wondered what coffee would be like with maple sugar in it. I wriggled back on the mattress so my back rested against the multitude of pillows on the bed. I wrapped my hands around the mug of coffee and decided I would try to listen without opening my mouth. I was getting better at it. I needed practice. That's all. Practice.

"Shall we get down to business then?" Iggie set his mug down and rubbed his hands together. "I've had enough coffee. I'll be pissing over the rail all day if I have more of it. I'm guessing you want to know why they let those Maudits anglais go free. Uh. Excuse me. Those Damned English."

"My main concern is, do Gabbie and Sebastien know what we are really up to?"

"I don't think so. But there is always a but, isn't there?"

"Damn."

"I said I don't *think* so. Gabbie Grenier is an honorable and compassionate man. I trust that if he learned about our real plan, he'd never say a word to anyone. Not even to Sebastien. As you know, Sebastien's not the most charitable."

"But they are close friends. In addition, Gabbie has absolutely no real personal interest in keeping quiet. The plan has nothing to do with protecting Acadia, which he has sworn to do."

"Ha ha, Hermel—Edward. If we carry out our plans. If we start this thing. You do not think Acadia will be in any danger when they find out?"

Start this thing? What thing? What was I missing? We had already started. Ah. But Monsieur St-Amand had said he had "business" in Boston.

"True enough. True enough." There was nothing even close to a smile on Monsieur St-Amand's face when he said this. All I saw was worry. No. Not worry. It was pure fear.

I understood little of what Monsieur St-Amand and Iggie were saying. They spoke on and on about "them." Whoever "them" was, it wasn't Jenny and Little Cock and me they were referring to. They whispered about the importance of helping "them" and of saving "their" lives. I could tell they wanted me to think they were speaking of Acadians but I knew they weren't. Not entirely, at least. They were speaking of strangers. Men and women they had never met but who were in great danger. The more I listened, the less I understood so I often drifted off into my own world. But the first time I heard an unfamiliar word—"entailed" was one of them—I took advantage and decided to stay awake and use the time as a learning opportunity. Both men were surprisingly good in English, at least it seemed to me they were, so until the midday meal arrived in the hands of Cabin Boy, I made myself into an apugji'j, a mouse, and listened and learned.

One thing I did understand perfectly was why the men at the fort had let Benny, Merit and Jacques l'Itale go. Iggie said they let them out of the jail so they would leave Acadia and go back to where they came from. Benny and his fellows were not the least bit interested in returning with an escaped female slave, they were there to learn about the lay of the land.

They already knew how much equipment, how many soldiers and weapons were in the area. This was common knowledge to anyone who docked near Port Royal and freely given to anyone sharing a table in the inn over mugs of rum or beer.

It seemed to me, though, that Monsieur St-Amand and Iggie were more worried about Gabbie Grenier and Sebastien Preux finding out about what they were calling "The Plan."

Monsieur St-Amand grunted that letting Benny go was a very good idea as long he and his cohorts "get the hell out of Acadia" and "go back to where they came from as fast as possible" before they learned there was more going on.

How had Gabbie Grenier planned to have them leave? How would these Damned English be leaving Acadia? On Captain KrommeZee's ship? Iggie explained it away for me: "How could Gabbie have known that all of *you* would be on KrommeZee's cursed ship? He was hoping and praying the whole maudit lot would be drowned at sea. Perhaps by some… some dreadful mischance?" A smile passed between the men.

"Ah," said Monsieur St-Amand. "Excellent. I am pleased to hear that he doesn't know the true purpose of Captain Kromme—"

A knock at the door came just as I was about to learn the one thing that would cause everything else to make sense. It was Cabin Boy. Right on time. End of learning opportunity.

Iggie and Monsieur St-Amand bowed heads to each other and Iggie left. The meal was for two. Master and slave. Cabin Boy placed dishes and bowls and cups, a bottle of wine and a teapot on the table then the last piece removed from his huge silver tray was one plate. This he handed to me.

On this plate was a dried up fish that smelled awful and two biscuits. "What's this?" I asked and received a sight of teeth, pulled-back lips and fierce eyebrows from Monsieur St-Amand from behind Cabin Boy. I made my glance go to my feet. "Thank you so much for your kindness. Um. Young Master." I forced a smile and was glad Cabin Boy wasn't able to see it properly from this angle. I'm sure he would have been frightened. "Much appreciated." I couldn't bring myself to call him "master" again so hoped its absence would go unnoticed.

As soon as Cabin Boy left I raised my eyes to Monsieur St-Amand and approached his table from under my own eyebrows and with my plate at arm's length. "Rotten fish? They expect me to eat rotten fish?"

"It's pickled herring. Seafarers' food."

"It stinks. I can't eat this? *Eesh.*" I was still holding my plate at arm's length.

Using his spoon and knife together, Monsieur St-Amand lifted one of several pieces of flat pink meat from a platter in the middle of the table. "Lower your plate. Here. Let me. Let me do this. Give it to me."

"But what if it touches the fish?"

He laughed like I'd never heard him laugh before. His head went back and nothing but pure joy came out of him. "Dump the offending food onto my plate."

I did. The fish and biscuits slid off to settle beside the eggs and cheese already there.

He placed the pink meat on mine.

"What is this?"

"Ham." He lifted the lid from one of the bowls and with a large spoon scooped out one egg. "Set your plate down. Right there." He placed the egg on my plate then scooped out a second one. "And these are eggs."

"I know what eggs are," I snapped. "I'm not stupid. I've just never seen most of this… this… whatever it all is." I recalled Claude's description of his meals at the estate of Philibert de Villegaignon, the Marquis de Savoie. I was beginning to put my imagination and memory to what lay before me. "But I've certainly heard of a lot of it."

Using his spoon and knife, Monsieur St-Amand sawed a piece of the pink meat off my piece, then held it out to me on the end of his knife. "Just try it. One little piece won't kill you."

I leaned down and took the meat into my mouth. Salty and sweet, tasting of my beloved maple syrup and something else. "It's been smoked?"

"Hickory."

"It's good. Give me another piece."

Monsieur St-Amand cut off another piece and put it into my mouth. "I don't mind feeding you but I would prefer to eat my own meal while it's still hot. Cold eggs aren't pleasant."

I snatched my plate and napkin-wrapped spoon and knife from the table and scurried toward the bed to eat.

"Please. Join me at the table."

I did, hoping he would tell me what his conversation with Iggie was about but he refused to say anything except: "It's better for you that you don't know until it's necessary to know. Will you forgive me?"

"What choice do I have?"

"None, I suppose."

A light rap on the door made me grab my plate and my mug of tea and head for the bed again.

"Enter."

Captain KrommeZee poked his head around the door as he slowly opened it. He looked first at Monsieur St-Amand, then at me. My face must have showed something because he asked: "Am I interrupting something?" He was smiling and I didn't like that. I was happy he didn't stay long and even happier to get some actual information from his brief talk with Monsieur St-Amand. He chose not to take a seat but instead, stood over Monsieur St-Amand as he spoke, occasionally going to the window to look out onto the sea. "We're heading into some rough seas so

I can't stay below. I'm needed at the helm."

I learned that Captain KrommeZee was transporting not only maple sugar and syrup from several villages in the area around Port Royal, but most importantly, wheat from the Big Meadow to the port at Salem and to Boston Harbor. There was money to be made. A great deal of it, so the farmers in the Boston area were not happy with imported wheat. In fact, "The whole of New England wants to either destroy us or take us over. They won't stand for anything less."

"I'm fully aware of that, Willem. And why I was so reluctant to take this trip right now. Believe me, Boston is the very last place I want to be these days. How many more ships are in the making?"

"Not nearly enough. We need money. Lots of it. And they are becoming even more suspicious than ever. That's my big worry."

"I had a chance last night to explore your ship…"

When was that? I wondered. I was a very light sleeper. He couldn't possibly have gotten out of his big chair and opened the door of the cabin without having me hear him. Unless. That last cup of tea. Did Monsieur St-Amand put something in it to make me sleep deeply? The next time he left the cabin, I would search his belongings.

"Very well designed, my friend. If I hadn't known what was disguised behind the cargo bulkheads, I would never have guessed. Our charges will be more than comfortable, bless their souls."

"How many more of your design wait for service in Île Royale?"

"Not nearly enough."

"How many, Willem!"

"Four."

"Four like these. We can move dozens in that case. You can't imagine how hap—"

My mouth opened and despite my promise to myself, this came out: "Dozens of what? What are you—? Sorry."

A fast glance went from Monsieur St-Amand to Captain KrommeZee.

Captain KrommeZee smiled at me. I didn't like this smile any more than I had the last one. "Cannons. War materiel. We must always be prepared for invasion." He turned back to Monsieur St-Amand. "You know yourself that this lady," he pointed at the floor, "this ship, is one of a kind. Were you not aware that the ships at Île Royale are war ships."

"I suppose I had hoped."

"They are small, swift, full of cannon and that's what we need so much money for. Damned cannons and shot. Delivered surreptitiously because they're watching us. That bastard Benjamin Church actually came on his own to spy on us. Can you believe the audacity of that… that…?" He looked at me again. "I won't use that word in the presence of a lady."

Monsieur St-Amand removed his napkin from his lap, wiped his mouth with it, then placed it beside his plate. "I admire determination and brilliance in a man but deplore it in an enemy."

"What did Iggie have to say? Anything enlightening? Anything that holds the slightest bit of relief for us? Worry-wise, I mean?"

"He ensured me that Grenier and Preux would have those bastards on board the next ship leaving the port. Or…" Monsieur St-Amand raised an invisible musket to his shoulder.

"The next ship means they are one day behind us. The weather ahead will slow us down. I pray they run into it, too. We can't have them boarding this ship for any reason."

Monsieur St-Amand poured two glasses of wine, one of which he lifted up to Captain KrommeZee. "Sit. Have a glass. I see there's a chess set in the cupboard there. Play a game?"

"Thanks, my friend, but I will need all my faculties in the next while. Drink both, or share with your delightful companion here."

He looked at me with that sly smile again. Did he really believe there was something going on between Monsieur St-Amand and me?

"Regardless, I must be on my way. If you pray, lovely lady, please pray that our enemies have caught that next ship. If they choose not to leave, they will die in Acadia and the whole of New England, soldiers and common man alike, will invade our land searching for their precious Major Benjamin Church. Well known, well liked. Although I have no idea why! And well respected as their protector and savior. I must bid you a good afternoon and a pleasant evening."

At the door he paused. "If you already know how to play chess, lovely lady, you will find a most challenging opponent in Edward Gooden here. If not, you will be instructed by a master." He laughed. "A different kind of master, of course!"

With the pointing finger of his right hand he touched his forehead and left.

With purposely slitted eyes, I glared at Monsieur St-Amand. "Just how long have you two known each other, anyway? Master?"

Fifteen

That evening, I went up onto the deck by myself because Monsieur St-Amand was snoring so loudly I couldn't think. And I had a lot to think about. One of the things being what had happened before he fell asleep. With my help. Yes. That afternoon, I had found his store of sleeping powders in his traveling bag and had slipped a packet into his last glass of wine. For his sake as much as for mine.

"I love you, Keskoua. I need you. I don't ever want to lose you. Please. Join me in the bed. We have only so much time to be together. I'm so sorry. I know you want to be with me."

"What are you talking about, Monsieur St-Amand?"

"I think of you constantly. I can't get you out of my mind. Please."

I had seen our people on the drink before and sometimes crying for a small reason built up into a big one, but Monsieur St-Amand had always seemed so sure of himself, confident, kind, even fatherly to me even though I knew in my heart that he was in love with me. And had always been, just as he was saying. And just as Jenny had told me the first day of the voyage: "You know he's in love with you, don't you."

I suppose I knew. But inside I knew something else. No. I didn't. I didn't know this something else for certain. I couldn't believe for one moment that Monsieur St-Amand could be so very cruel as to let me believe that he loved only me, to actually love only me, but be able to stop it just like that.

I knew he had always held himself back from me both before and after Falcon became my husband because he was not yet divorced from his wife in France. He had told me often how she had deceived him, how she had taken up with another man, had even given the other man a child, a child that bore the St-Amand name because that's the way the Law dictated it. A child took the name of the husband whether he was the father or not. It was a boy child so would inherit Monsieur St-Amand's estate, such as it was. Monsieur St-Amand had told me many times that he could take no other woman as a wife, could love no other woman, could make love to no other woman until the divorce was finalized.

One moon earlier, he had received word that the divorce was final and showed me the papers that proved it. As I think back, he shared everything with me. The papers made no sense to me as the writing was full of thuses and therefores and with words I didn't know and didn't care to learn. He said it would be possible now for him to marry again in the Church because the marriage had been annulled. It was not a divorce.

The thought jumped into my head that if anything happened to Falcon, I would— No. I threw that thought away. It was wrong. But it comforted me just the same to know that I would not have to be alone if the worst thing came about.

It was soon afterwards that Monsieur St-Amand informed us that he would pay for our way to Boston as he had "business dealings" there. That I had to accompany our little group in order for him to do this for Jenny and Little Cock. I did not know that his "business dealings" had much to do with a new wife.

"Technically I could marry you," he told me, tears streaming down his face. "Your marriage with Falcon was not blessed by the Church but you're hardly a virgin, are you?" He seemed to think this was particularly funny and his laugh shook the cabin. I'm sure everyone on board must have wondered what was happening between us.

"How old is your new bride, then? Twelve?"

"She is your age. In fact, one year older."

"She must be very ugly if she is my age and no one has loved her yet."

"She is not ugly. Not at all. She is perfect." His eyes sought a far corner of the cabin as he drifted off to a place I was not at all welcome to join him at. "Perfect."

Feelings rushed into me that were so strong, I wasn't sure I could survive another moment without jumping off the ship into the mouth of a shark.

After a few moments, he came back. "So what say you, *Dawn*?"

Using my slave name seemed to bring something unpleasant out of him. Something I'd never seen in him before. It made me feel sick inside.

"Shall I exercise my owner's privilege and order you to satisfy my need of you? I know you love me. I know you want me. Nobody will know. They all think it anyway. Have you not seen how all the men look at you? You're so beautiful. I've always desired you. Even the times I went away to be with other women."

"To Mirligueche?" I guess as long as you didn't love them, you were allowed to make love to them after all.

"Yes. And other places. But no matter where I went, I could think only of you when they were servicing me. In my heart of hearts, I wanted it to be you doing those things. Don't you see how much I love you?"

I was beginning to fear this man I had trusted with my very life for so many years. Who was he? He was not the man I had known. Something had changed in him. Something deep inside had broken. What had broken him so badly? How many secrets did this man have?

"I know you will give me much more than she ever can and that breaks my heart. My heart is broken. What terrible mistakes I've made. Come to my bed. Let me love you before it's too late. Let us love each other until the last moment before I must bid you adieu. I will always hold you in my heart."

"She will be returning to Port Royal with you?"

"No. She would never adapt to that kind of life. She's a lady."

"You mean…"

"Yes. I'll be staying in Boston."

"I'll never see you again." I was not seeing *him* again in the first place. The man I had known and loved and secretly desired was no longer inside this person sitting on the edge of the bed pleading with me to share my body with him.

"I will ensure that you always have a supply of pigeons."

"Pigeons!"

"Yes. Pigeons. Weeks quicker than messages by ship. Months quicker than by land. Write small and on thin paper and one can communicate heart and soul to a beloved." His thoughts drifted away to the corner of the cabin again.

Mine drifted to the sleeping powders inside his cupboard.

He patted the bed beside him. "Come. I know you want me. You've always wanted me, haven't you?"

"Let me get your sleeping shirt from your cupboard first. Then one more glass of wine for you."

And this is what brought me onto the main deck after dark where I caused the death of Gregor.

Sixteen

I think the most difficult task in life is to mourn the loss of a loved one when he is still alive. The most basic fear in a human being—present at birth—is the fear of falling. The second is the fear of abandonment, strongest at the age of two winters. The greatest assurance in all of us is hope. Take that away and we are no longer human.

I was enraged by the time I got to the deck. Gregor was on watch. No one else was around. He approached me, ran his eyes over me. What was it with these men! And reached to touch my left breast.

"He sent ye up for me, did he now?"

I cringed. Stepped back from him. "Touch me like that again and you'll be shark food."

"Ah. The little lady has some fire. I like that."

He reached out again but this time, he was quick and turned me around with my back to him so he could cover my mouth with one hand as he put his other hand over my breast. He squeezed hard. It hurt. I screamed beneath his hand. I banged my feet on the deck hoping to arouse the attention of anyone below. It would not be Monsieur St-Amand who came to my rescue. He was drunk and drugged. I wriggled and struggled as best I could but Gregor was much too strong.

I was about to relax and let him think I had agreed to his demands when he cried out and slumped away from me and landed hard on the deck. I turned to see Jenny, blood dripping from the knife in her hand.

"*Bastardo estuprar maldito,*" she spat at him. "*I deve cortar seu pênis.*"

Staring up at Jenny while trying to reach around behind his own back, Gregor groaned. "Whore. What did you do to me?"

"It's what we're going to do." She tossed the bloody knife toward the rail and bent down to grasp one of his feet. "Come on, Keskoua. Grab his other leg." She began to pull him toward the rail. I helped.

She must have connected with one of his lungs because Gregor's breathing became more labored. He tried to call out but coughed instead. Blood came out of his mouth.

"Move the gangplank away from the gate," I whispered to her.

She did. It made a much louder sound than I expected. We both held our breath and didn't move for three breaths.

A shout from below. "What's happening up there, Gregor, y'idjit? Lookin' for hidden rum?" A laugh.

Gregor tried to answer but another coughing fit took him over. His pleading eyes sought mine but I looked away. I whispered "Hurry."

Jenny stopped. She let Gregor's leg go and stood to her full height. I turned to see what—I knew it would be a who—she was looking at.

Woodpecker Food.

"Aye. And what have you ladies done here?" From the hips he leaned over as far as his wooden leg would allow to peer into Gregor's face. "And what did you do to deserve it? Ah. No need to answer that." He looked up at Jenny then at me. "Which one of you lovely ladies did he go grabbin' for?" He stood up straight. "Doesn't matter. Let's get this garbage overboard before anyone else comes along. Grab a leg each again, ladies."

Woodpecker Food took hold of Gregor's left arm and the three of us dragged Gregor to the rail and over he went without a sound.

Woodpecker Food slid the gangplank back over the open gate. "Mops are in the hold. You'll need to clean up the blood. What did you use to incapacitate him, hé?"

Jenny pointed at the bloody knife lying below a row of neatly coiled ropes hanging from pegs along the rail.

Woodpecker Food picked it up, examined it briefly. "It's a good one. Pity." Over the side it went. "I'll go below and hand up the mops and keep anybody from comin' up here until ye're done."

He disappeared below. After a few moments, his head popped up along with two mops and a pail of soapy water. "Be quick about it." His head disappeared again, then up it came. "And ladies…"

We turned to look at him. Jenny's face was as pale as it could be with her dark skin. Her cheeks were hollow.

"Ye did the world a favor. Don't lose sleep over the likes of him." Head down then back up again. "Just dump the bucket over the side and ye can leave the mops on the deck."

"Thank you," I said.

"More'n welcome, ladies. Never warmed up to the man. What I'll do is watch for when yer done and come up to check on something I heard that woke me. Will that suit ye?"

I looked over at Jenny who was scrubbing the deck where Gregor had first gone down with every bit of strength she had in her body. "It will," I said and started scrubbing from the rail in.

Seventeen

I had slept in the big chair in the cabin but every time Monsieur St-Amand stirred or grunted or rolled onto his back to resume his snoring, I would wake up. And light was coming in through the crack in the cabin's curtains. I didn't want to believe it was morning. I didn't want to believe the night I'd had either. Maybe it had been a melgwisgat, a nightmare. No. It was no nightmare. It had been real. I adjusted my blanket and switched sides. I was beginning to know what a baby must feel curled up inside its mother shortly before deciding to come out into the world. I was everything but upside down trying to get comfortable inside this deep cushioned chair.

I had just closed my eyes and started to drift off into thoughts of some of that tasty pink ham for the morning meal when thunder made me jump right up out of my chair.

Monsieur St-Amand sat up straight, grabbed his forehead in both hands, groaned, threw his feet onto the floor, pulled the chamber pot from under his bed and emptied his stomach.

Thunder again. At the door. Someone wanted in. Men's voices. I recognized Little Cock's and I think Bosselé, too. I opened the door.

"What do y—?"

Bosselé had Woodpecker Food by the shoulder of his shirt. He dragged him into the room, turned to Little Cock: "Get in here!"

Little Cock, looking sadder than I'd seen him for days, stepped in.

"And shut the focking door."

The door was shut and the three of them stood there.

From beside me: "Jésus-Christ sur la croix. Qu'est-ce au nom du Dieu Tout-Puissant qui se passe?"

"Exactly what I want to know." Bosselé's glare told me he knew all about Gregor's unplanned swim in the ocean. "Well?"

From beside me a groan. "Oh, Kes— Dawn. I'm so sorry. I'm so very sorry. I shouldn't have said that. Any of that."

I snapped at him, "So that makes it not true then?" I snapped at Bosselé, "What's your problem?" From the arm of the big chair I took a housecoat and slipped my arms into it. I tied it tight. "What's going on?"

"The very question I have for you. You and your cohort down in the slave quarters. What the hell happened last night?"

"I—"

Woodpecker Food stepped in front of Bosselé. Woody was going to defend me against a man over a head taller than he? "Leave her alone. I'll explain."

Beside me, "Oh, God," and more retching.

"Serves you right for lying."

"I'm not lying."

"If you were not lying last night, you're lying this morning. Choose your lie. Then live with it."

"Can we possibly get back to the business at hand you two?"

"He's got nothing to do with it," I said pointing at Monsieur St-Amand. "Well, indirectly perhaps."

"Make sense, girl. I know you were up on deck. After dark. Asking for trouble from Gregor when you know full well what he's like."

"Ask for it? *Ask for it?* Are you seriously saying I wanted that… that… that… *creature* to touch me?" There was no word in my language to describe him. "*Ai!*"

"Avast, Dawn. Avast. I understand why you might have been upset."

"Upset? UPSET? It feels like the whole ship is wanting me to spread my legs. What am I? Property? Chattel?"

From beside me: "Technically on this voyage…"

"And you! Not another WORD from you!" I shook my finger at him. "Master!"

"Just hand me that jug of water and a glass. Please."

"Get it yourself." I whirled back to the men. Bosselé and Woodpecker Food had stepped back by two paces.

Little Cock looked up at me. "He was the only one who knew for certain where Lilac went to." Tears came. I wrapped my arms around him and patted his back like he was a child awakened from a melgwisgat.

"Let's all sit. I have something to say," said Bosselé.

"I can't bear to hear it again." Little Cock escaped from my arms to slip out the door into the passageway.

***

Bosselé began.

"I went only as far as the first tavern. I didn't go with Gregor and Pêssegos to sell the girl. I was too busy getting serviced by one of the ladies there. I don't know which inn for sure they sold her at. Or even if it was an inn. Or even if they didn't take advantage of her, kill her and toss her away somewhere like garbage. I can only go by what they told Captain when they returned.

"Ever since then, though, every time a ship I was working on docked in this harbor, I went ashore and asked question after question, trying to do what I could to find out what had happened to LC's sister. I mean Pierce's sister."

No one corrected Bosselé on his slip of Little Cock's former pirate name. We were all stressed for one reason or another. Behind me, I heard

Monsieur St-Amand pouring himself a glass of water.

"The only place where I got no information from—whatsoever—was the Blind Pig Inn. In fact, any time I stopped there to ask questions, the owner… I believe his name was Waite. Brian Waite. Yes. He would make a motion with his eyes and a couple of fellows—really big Black fellows—would step up to the desk, one on either side of me and he would ask: 'What is it again you're ferreting around about?'

"A few times, I saw a girl there that he claimed was his daughter. Hard to believe that. She had Indian features. The Puritans in that area are adamantly opposed to mixed-race marriages. She would be around twenty-five now. Last time I saw her, she was perhaps nineteen. Old man Waite had died and she was running the inn. From what I heard, successfully, too. But we have no *sure* way of knowing if she is the daughter of Lilac. I asked around and everyone I spoke to assured me that she was the daughter of Brian Waite with the wife he had at the time. None other." Bosselé shrugged. "But not a one of those I spoke to would look me in the eye when telling me these tales. Tell me what that tells you."

"We'll have Pierce check it out when we arrive in Boston," offered Monsieur St-Amand, his voice stronger. "Hurry up and get this story over with, Bosselé. I am desperate for food. Something on my stomach will quell my suffering."

"Had a bit of a night, did ye?" Woodpecker Food gave me a knowing glance. To me he said: "Now I understand a bit more your need to take the night air, Miss."

"Who is the girl, then?" asked Monsieur St-Amand. "Pierce's sister? No. She would be much older. Who?"

"I think it must be her daughter. Her daughter by Jacques l'Itale by the timing of things."

I gasped.

Monsieur St-Amand grunted something in French.

Woodpecker Food bowed his head and shook it slowly. "Sad story there."

"Died in childbirth."

"Does Little— Does Pierce know?"

Bosselé and Woodpecker Food nodded together. Bosselé said, "We had to tell him it was a possibility."

"A *probability*," said Woodpecker Food.

"He knew that Gregor had all the exact details. Pierce fell apart when he learned of Gregor's… Gregor's accident."

"What accident was that?" asked Monsieur St-Amand.

One side of Woodpecker Food's mouth went up in a half smile. "Seems a frightened and angry young lady took affront to his advances and her friend made him taste the blade. He's shark food."

From behind me, Monsieur St-Amand reached out to grab my shoulder to turn me around.

I shrugged away. "Think about what happened to the last man who touched me when I didn't want to be touched."

"I said I was sorry. I mean it. I'm sor—"

A knock at the cabin door made us all jump a bit.

Woodpecker Food opened it.

Nervously clutching a shiny blue housecoat closely around her in tight fists she said, "Something's wrong with…" She glanced at Woodpecker Food, then Bosselé, then me, then Monsieur St-Amand. "With Pierce. I think he's having a… *uma convulsão*. I don't know how to say it in English. His eyes. His eyes. They go away into his head. He's shaking. Come quickly."

"Merde," said Monsieur St-Amand. He opened his cupboard, grabbed a small bag from inside and rushed into the passageway behind Jenny.

"Quickly," she said. "This way."

It seemed to me that there was more going on with Jenny than Little Cock's fit. I would check in on both of them later. We were about to dock in Salem.

Eighteen

Woodpecker Food came up behind me just as the ship was sliding into the dock at the port in Salem. I was watching the side of the ship as it came within a bear's hair length of the dock without touching it—our Captain wasn't so bad a pilot after all—so I wasn't expecting an arm across my back and a body pressing into my side as though we'd been sleeping on the cedars together all our lives.

"What are you doing?" I said, twirling away from his grasp. Ropes and pulleys snaked down into the hold behind him as some of the crew prepared to lift what I knew would be large bundles of wheat from the Big Meadow. With the stress of what they were putting into their task, not one of them glanced over at Woodpecker Food and me. They usually kept a good eye out anytime any of the crew came around me after what had happened to Gregor. Word had spread quickly that I wasn't one to be messed with.

"What? Nothing. I'm just..." His breath smelled like last night's rum. "I'm just being friendly. We're friends, right?" And he reached out to put his arm over my shoulders again.

"Don't touch me. Especially like that. What's wrong with you? You should know better."

Realization passed over his face and he stepped back. "Oh. Dawn. I'm sorry. I'm sorry. I just thought..." I could see through his wide apologetic grin that he had a mouth full of gold teeth. "It was a brotherly hug, that's all. I'm sorry. I thought we were… Ye know. All in this together now."

"We are but you are not my brother."

He reached out yet again I think to pat my shoulder then shook both hands in the air.

"Belay that, Woodpecker Food." The Captain's voice came loud over the activities on our deck and on the dock below where men shifted huge packages wrapped in heavy cloth and ropes over to where the gangplank would be. "Help Bosselé with the gangplank. We're in port. Haven't you noticed? Or are you still drunk and dreaming?"

An ever-so-gentle bump of ship against dock shuffled Woodpecker Food and me apart enough for me to scurry away while Captain cursed Woodpecker Food with words I'd never heard before. Other crew laughed as he passed them, then went back to their individual chores.

Muscles bulging with the weight of the gangplank, Bosselé raised his eyebrows at me in a question. I shrugged at him then turned away to go below. I needed to see if Monsieur St-Amand had been able to help Little Cock through his fit. And to see if there was more going on with Jenny.

On the way down, Monsieur St-Amand and I met at the ladder on the second deck, me going down, him coming up. I was two steps down it and him only one up so he removed his hands from the rails, stepped down and moved back. In doing so, he made a slight gentlemanly bow of his upper body. Cabin Boy, just coming out of the kitchen with Captain's tall brown mug on a tray, steaming, noticed this action of Monsieur's and a sly smile spread over his lower face as he looked at me. His gaze tore all the way through my apron, bodice and shift then lowered to go through my petticoats and pantaloons. During the summers in my village I wore little, but with this young man's eyes on me, I had never felt more naked in my life. When my feet touched, I moved to the other side of Monsieur St-Amand and pressed myself against the bulkhead so the boy wouldn't be able to brush against me when he went up the ladder with Captain's tray.

In a stern voice, Monsieur St-Amand said to me, "I must go ashore. Pierce is fine now but for some reason, Jenny seems upset about something now. Perhaps his fit frightened her."

"That's where I'm going. I noticed her unease, too. I mean, yes, very well, Master. As you wish. Would you please ask Captain if he might have something—other than rum—that might calm her if indeed she needs calming? Uh. Please. Master."

Monsieur St-Amand's hand went to his forehead and he glanced over at me from under it and tried to make his face stern although I could see a smile pulling at one corner of his mouth. "Don't overdo it," he whispered. Then with authority: "I have many more important things on my mind. See to it yourself."

I bent my knees in a quick little motion and looked at him with my eyelashes beating together. I did not smile. "Yes, Master."

Monsieur St-Amand brought his lips into his mouth and pinched them with his teeth, but the laugh came out of his eyes anyway. I was glad that his hand still shielded most of his face from the view of the cook who was now watching us. Monsieur whispered *Stop that,* then in a loud voice again said, "Well get to it then. Time's a-wasting."

***

Even though the skin was tight over her bones and she had to hold her cup of water with both hands while she drank from it, Jenny wasn't ill. What she was, was filled with fear. And not fear of having seen Little Cock's fit. It was much more than that and it had something to do with our arrival in Salem. When I told her that it always helps if you put your fears out on the blanket in front of you so you can see them for what they really are, she gave me that special warning look of hers: Stop asking.

I stopped.

As it turned out, I would not need to ask Jenny any more about herself as someone who was more than willing to talk and talk and talk about what had happened to her soon came into the lives of everyone on the ship.

"I'm going up," I told Little Cock and Jenteg. "Think about what I said. Talking about your fears, I mean. Little Cock is a good listener and he cares for you."

He nodded.

"It will do him good to share things of his own, too, while he recovers from his relapse. Am I right, Little Cock?"

He smiled. "More water, Jenny?"

***

As I reached the second deck and was about to put my hand on the ladder leading to the main deck, I met Cabin Boy on his way down it. On his tray was Captain's clay mug no longer steaming, so empty. Clay mugs were breakable, I knew. And I also knew it was Captain's favorite. As Cabin Boy reached the last step on the ladder, I dipped my knees even lower than I'd done with Monsieur St-Amand so I could spread the material of my long skirt below his descending foot.

I waited until his full weight was on my skirt, the only foot carrying his weight, then… "Oh, my goodness." I smiled and fluttered my eyelashes. "There is so little room to pass each other here, isn't there?"

I took a fast and long step up and back, pulling my skirt—and therefore his foot—along with it.

Down he went with a curse and a crash of Captain's favorite clay mug.

"Oh, you poor thing," I said in my best English. "Are you quite all right?"

I didn't understand the words coming out of *his* mouth, either. I tossed my skirt over one shoulder and scampered up the ladder like a squirrel teasing her mate.

When I reached the deck, Bosselé, who was doing something to the sails along with Woodpecker Food—folding them, I think, I didn't know the right term—closed one eye and motioned with his head for me to look over at the ship's rail closest to the dock.

I didn't know it yet, but the one who would be so willing to talk and talk and talk about Jenny came in the person of a short, wide woman who made her way up the gangplank as though it was a log across a spring stream. She was snuffling into a huge handkerchief and crying like she planned to flood the main deck with her tears when she got there. The hand not holding her handkerchief was on her white bonnet. As she reached the top of the gangplank and removed that hand from her bonnet to grasp the ship's rail to hoist herself onto the deck, a strong wind suddenly lifted her cape high above her shoulders. A following gust spiraled her bonnet off and sent it down into the rubbish-filled seawater that was licking at the dock's supports. With her black cape flowing behind her like wings and her red hair secured high on the top of her head, she reminded me of an apo'qajej, a woodpecker. I covered my mouth with my hand as I wondered how she and Woodpecker Food would get along during the voyage.

The woman's *wings* flapped against the hatless man behind her. A hat's brim would have protected part of his face at least. He scowled, not at her, but with concentration, and he made no attempt to protect his down-turned face from the slaps of her cape. His hands were too busy. They slid along the gangplank's ropes tightly enough to cause both rope-slivers and blisters. When she stopped, he bumped into her and lost his balance, which made the rope he fell against go back and forth with his weight. He nearly went over into the spoils below where the woman's bonnet floated. He quickly recovered and looked up and ahead. This allowed me to see his face: cheeks a dark sick orangey pink and whites of blue eyes the same color as the woman's hair. I hoped Woodpecker Food had told the truth about the vast store of rum on board. I had a feeling this man would make a large hole in the supply during the next part of our voyage.

The woman began: "What a dreadful stench the sea has this morning and I've lost my bonnet." She stepped onto the deck and turned. "Oh, my darling. It seems I've lost my pretty bonnet. Go fetch it for me. Please?" She tilted her head to one side and her fluttering eyelashes put my attempts to shame. She snuffled and made a great noise of crying as she stepped farther onto the deck. Her black cape had settled back around her body like folded wings.

Looking into the faces of the men who had stopped doing everything and were standing there somewhere between amazement and amusement, she said, "What a friendly group you are. All smiles for me in my terribly sad state. I've lost my half-sister, you know. Terrible, terrible. We weren't close. I think I met her only once and that only briefly, but family is family, isn't it? You men, of all people, must understand how important a loving family is, seeing as you have none of your own with you, and you're away for months at a time."

Tommy looked over at Lars and raised one eyebrow. Lars turned his back and pretended to fix a rope on the far rail but I could see his shoulders shaking with silent laughter.

The woman looked down and plucked at her cape to smooth it. "You appear to be the most intelligent man on board, you must be the captain. I'll need someone to bring my trunks up."

Captain KrommeZee stepped forward with hands behind his back and a low bow to greet the woman but she stepped up to Bosselé.

Behind Bosselé, Lars had managed to control himself so was now watching what was going on. But he lost control again. His escaping laugh was muffled by a rough voice calling out from the gangplank. "I canna be holding this cargo up for the whole day. Can ya move yer arse? Turn around and go up ya stupid goose ya."

The woman glanced around to see what might be causing the commotion. She didn't realize that her man was attempting to descend the gangplank, but was blocked by a short, skinny dock worker with a bundle on his bent back that was three times larger than he was. It had to be balls of wound wool; we were to be taking some on, I'd heard. Perhaps some of it would make its way to Marguerite. Anything heavier would have broken him in half at that size.

"Belay that," said KrommeZee moving starboard and looking down, his scowl sending curious seabirds off the rail. "We've a load of wheat to go ashore before you start filling our decks. Back off."

The short, skinny man and the woman's man stood face to waist while the seabirds fluttered over their heads squawking as though to repeat Captain's orders. The short, skinny man shook his head, turned as though the load on his back was a bag of air and moved down the plank to the dock like a dancer with the woman's man following like a half-starved clumsy lumbering bear close behind him.

The woman waddled over to the rail "That's it there, honey-sop." The woman pointed to the floating mess. "There's my bonnet. I need it. I brought only the one."

The short, skinny man set down his burden on the dock and turned to Honey-Sop. "I take it ye can swim while yer holding yer nose against the stench of that *stront*?" He threw back his head and laughed.

I stepped forward. "I have an extra bonnet you can have. Uh, Miss."

The woman turned, removed her handkerchief from her nose, looked me down and up then down and up again. She snorted. "Just whom do you think you're speaking to?" Her handkerchief went back to her nose.

If I had bit my tongue any harder, the end of it would have dropped onto the deck. I did my little knee bend, tipped my head to one side with my eyes both lowered and batting at her at the same time. I was getting good at this subservience thing. "Apologies, Miss."

"Humph." She peered again down to where her man was. I now

assumed he was her husband as she would hardly have called a mere servant, honey-sop.

I felt someone beside me and flinched but it was Little Cock. "Good to see you up and about and feeling better."

"I heard we had travelers coming aboard."

Together, we peered over the rail to watch.

"What you told Jenny and me made her feel better. We talked," he said. "She's coming up for some fresh air." Little Cock sniffed. "Such as it is. At least it's somewhat sunny already."

I saw Bosselé move toward the ladder leading below decks and watched as he helped Jenny climb out. She hurried over to where Little Cock and I stood. Little Cock was right. She had not covered herself this time. The color had come back to her cheeks. She put her arm around my waist.

"What's going on?" She hadn't seen the woman yet.

"I can't wait to see this," Little Cock said.

Down below, Honey-Sop was as close to the edge of the dock as he could be. He was staring down through the narrow space between dock and ship at the dirty water there. He removed his jacket and after folding it carefully, he placed it on the dock. All activity had ceased on both ship and shore as everyone watched, no doubt wondering what this fool was going to do. He rolled up the left sleeve of his shirt exposing the thinnest arm I had ever seen on anything but bones left by a wolf pack. He bent slightly as though deciding to jump in.

The short, skinny man who, by this time, had moved his huge bundle a short distance away, stepped to a salt-coated wooden building whose near wall was hung with nets and oars, anchors and other equipment. He grasped a long pole with a vicious hook on one end of it.

"Here," he called out laughing. "Use this y'idjit." And he tossed it just as Honey-Sop turned toward the skinny man's voice.

Normal instinct would have caused a man to reach up with open hand to catch it—and it had been thrown with experience—but Honey-Sop instead curled one shoulder up to protect himself. (This made me wonder how many times he had to protect himself in the home of his beloved.) Jenny, Little Cock and I watched as the pole floated through the air, bumped against Honey-Sop's back, then tipped to imbed its hook briefly into his unprotected head. I saw a spurt of blood come out before his hand covered it. I knew the wound itself would not be a serious one, but I also knew that I did not have the medicines with me to prevent the sickness that would most certainly come from that wound. First, Jacques l'Itale, and now this man with a head injury. Were the Ancestors sending me a message about protecting the head by using what's in it? I hoped Monsieur would either have some medicines in his bag or that Captain would have something on board. Captain KrommeZee had not hired a surgeon.

The woman's scream made all three of us look up from dock to deck.

Jenny gasped. To Little Cock, she said, "That's the cow. That's the one. *A vaca imunda.*"

"What did you say?" I asked.

"It means filthy cow," Little Cock whispered.

Jenny growled, "Ela é a vaca imunda que arruinou a minha vida."

Both Little Cock and I hushed her. "Shh. Shh. Nothing but English. Remember? Shush."

"*Vaca!*" she screamed, but before she could throw herself at Vaca Imunda, Little Cock managed to cover her mouth, wrap his other arm around her and spirit her away down into the hold.

I had thought Vaca Imunda was too involved in her own predicament to notice. She began giving orders to Bosselé that he should: "Do something. Do something. My husband has been injured! You fools! Can't you see how distraught I am?" But then she turned to me. "Who was that who cried out to curse my husband? It was you, wasn't it?" The arm not holding her handkerchief was extended to its full length as she pointed at me. "Devil! She is a Devil. I saw an apparition beside her. She conjured it up to curse me and my husband. Devil!"

By this time, several men on the dock were tending to Honey-Sop who seemed to be bearing his injury well. They were helping him up the gangplank, one pulling, one pushing. I took a second look at what they had placed on his head to keep the blood from flowing over his clothing and was both worried and surprised to see that somebody had managed to catch Vaca Imunda's bonnet from the filthy water below and had used that.

I hope the medicines that Monsieur and Captain had would be strong ones. Honey-Sop would need it.

Nineteen

Because of all the fuss Vaca Imunda had caused over Honey-Sop and then over seeing Jenny beside me, full attention from everyone on shore was now on Captain KrommeZee's brand new, unchristened, unregistered ship.

The short, skinny man pointed to the ship's prow. "*There's no name on her! She has no name!*"

Three of his fellows had hoisted bundles onto their shoulders and had lined up to come aboard after Tommy and Lars finished debarking with their parcels of wheat from the Big Meadow, and the maple syrup from our village. But Skinny Man's fellows tossed aside their bundles and ran to the far side of the dock away from us.

They cried out as one: "CURSED SHIP. CURSED SHIP."

Skinny Man followed at their heels.

That's when I noticed that Monsieur St-Amand had returned from his errands. He had been almost knocked over by one of Skinny Man's fellows. He recovered his balance and looked up at me. From that distance, I could only guess what he was thinking. He pushed his way through the gathering crowd—even children were appearing: the girls' bonnets askew and chin ribbons flying and the boys' wide-brimmed flat hats held down or carried with one hand.

Vaca Imunda screamed "*I told you so! I told you so!*" and threw her arms around Honey-Sop, her cape covering him like a wing hiding him from view. She pointed at me. "That one's the Devil. She is the one who has cursed the ship. SHE HAS CURSED ALL OF US!"

It started as a murmur, but it soon appeared that everyone on the dock was screaming *BURN THE WITCH. BURN THE WITCH.* There had to be at least a hundred people jostling on the dock.

Beside me, Little Cock said: "Looks like the whole damned village has showed up for that woman's performance. Isn't she a piece of work?"

I nodded my head. "Monsieur St-Am—Master has returned. Perhaps he can give her something to quiet her down."

"Like a musket ball to the temple?"

I tried not to laugh but gave up and let one explode out of my mouth.

Vaca Imunda's glance sent my laugh into the air with the circling seabirds. I aimed my own glance at the ship's railing where it would cause no harm.

"Perhaps you should go below," Little Cock advised me. "It appears you are gaining even more attention now than she is. I know her kind. She is likely to be throwing the first sulfur stick on your pyre."

Below us on the dock, Tommy and Lars had unburdened themselves of the last of the wheat and syrup and were reaching for the big bundles of what I had learned was definitely spun wool. The bundles were large but light. No one looked at Tommy and Lars, the crowd on the dock was too intent on screaming out its fear at me. Then all our crew were quickly descending and ascending the gangplank with cargo and Captain KrommeZee was among them. Monsieur St-Amand hoisted a bundle onto his shoulders on the way up to the deck and carried it to where Bosselé and Woodpecker Food were sending the packages below into the hold. As they lowered bundles and raised empty ropes, they shouted encouragement to whoever was down there.

When Monsieur St-Amand turned away to go back down to the dock for another bundle, Bosselé grabbed his arm. He spoke quietly but I heard every word. "The crew can handle it, Hermel. They're used to working together under pressure so will do it in no time. Adding you into the mix might cause an accident as you are not used to working with this crew. We cannot afford a delay. The lady there is in danger." Bosselé indicated me with the top of his head. "Deal with the real witch, will you?"

Monsieur St-Amand turned to us. "Pierce, take Dawn below. Stay in my cabin with her until I myself come fetch you. Understand?"

"Understood, Master." Little Cock pushed me toward the ladder.

***

An uproar from above took Little Cock and me from our half-sleep to full awareness of where we were: Monsieur St-Amand's cabin. The last things I remembered were being sent below with him by "Master," feeling the jolt caused by the wind catching the sails as we sped away from the port at Salem, and the angry voices from the dock squawking along with the seabirds. The light from the cabin's windows told me it was halfway closer to sunset than to midday. We'd been below for a long time.

A tap on the cabin door caused Little Cock and me to look at each other with worry. We stared, unmoving, as the handle of the door turned. But the door eased open and Monsieur St-Amand's head appeared like a squirrel's from behind a tree. "You fellows awake?" He stepped inside. "You can't miss this. That woman is still complaining. Somebody's going to end up throwing her overboard."

We hurried up to the deck and Little Cock and I hid ourselves behind a cluster of hanging loops of rope. The sea was fairly calm so they didn't sway too much so we were able to take in the whole scene. Someone had placed out three wooden boxes and covered them with extra sail cloth. Two mismatched candlesticks—empty—sat on the cloth along with knives and spoons, plates heaped with the simple fare we had been eating since leaving Port Royal, and dishes and bowls of things I was not familiar with. Several chairs (they were likely Captain KrommeZee's cabin chairs) had been set up and two of them contained Vaca Imunda and Honey-Sop, Vaca's mouth moving, not with eating, but with talking. Honey-Sop's concentration was on consuming from his left hand a biscuit, from his right hand, rum right from the bottle. He set neither of them down while doing this: a bite of biscuit, four chews, three swallows of rum, a bite of biscuit, four chews, three swallows of rum. I saw that one exhausted bottle of rum lay on its side with a tiny pool of brown fluid beneath its lip. Both Honey-Sop and Vaca had napkins tucked into their neck pieces and had empty plates before them. Honey-Sop's head had been wrapped with what I hoped were clean strips of cloth.

With the little finger of her right hand sticking out slightly and delicately curled, Vaca lifted the bottom end of her napkin to pat her pursed lips. She let the napkin's end escape back to its place on her bosom, then she reached for the handle of a delicate cup to her right—I guessed there was tea in it—little finger still impossibly curled. Then she sipped. At the same time as her lips curled down, her curled little finger went up like a mulumgwej, a groundhog, coming out of his hole first thing in the morning to check for danger. She turned toward Honey-Sop, her voice like that of a fisher cat (she was a strange beast). "DISGUSTING!"

Although Honey-Sop's ear was closer to her mouth than a fisher cat from nose to tail, he made no indication that he had heard her, not even a single flutter of eyelashes. I wondered if the blow to his head with the bonnet catcher had damaged his hearing. On the other side of her, Cabin Boy, removing empty platters and bowls from the canvas, winced and squeezed his near eye into a slit. At the end of the makeshift table, Bosselé lifted up the front of his shirt to hide his laugh behind it.

Vaca continued. "You people know *nothing* of proper culinary deport—"

As Monsieur St-Amand tried to go quietly to the stern of the boat where Captain KrommeZee stood behind the wheel, he stepped into her field of vision.

"Well there you are. Where did you disappear to, silly boy? Come dine with us."

Monsieur St-Amand bowed graciously and smiled. He rubbed his hand across his stomach. "I fear I have no appetite for food, m'lady." And he scurried away.

She graced the crew with a tight smile of understanding then dabbed it away with her napkin. "What say I tell you an after meal story about how I saved my village from the Devil himself?"

Several crew turned to just-remembered tasks and others headed for the ladder leading to below deck but Captain KrommeZee, obviously in a jovial mood, called out. "By all means. I'm sure we would ALL enjoy some rare entertainment by a lady such as yourself *isn't that right, gentlemen?*"

Stowing their grumbles, the crew returned to the makeshift table and settled in, some sitting cross-legged on the deck, others sitting zigzag on the steps leading up to the ship's wheel where Monsieur St-Amand and Captain KrommeZee remained, and some standing, leaning elbow on rail.

***

"I saw her, you know. I saw her apparition beside that Indian Devil who was up here on the top floor earlier today when my dear husband was so severely injured." Vaca Imunda dabbed her eyes with a handkerchief with red and purple flowers on it.

"Her name was Tituba and she's dead now. Thank the Good Lord for that. Beautiful. Too beautiful. God cursed her beauty by covering it with black skin. Serves her right, don't you think?"

A polite mumble.

"Well I fixed her, didn't I?"

Beside me, Little Cock leaned in to whisper. "It looks like we are finally going to get to the bottom of that mess that started in Salem."

"What mess?" I whispered back.

"Hanged a couple dozen folks. And they crushed one old man under a pile of stones. Can you imagine?"

I couldn't.

"Well maybe it wasn't quite that many. Stories vary. But others went to jail and died there."

"What happened?"

"The children. The children took fits and they blamed it all on that Tituba woman she just mentioned."

"Because she was beautiful?"

"These people are not like us, Kes— uh, Dawn. They have these really strange ideas in their heads about how life works. Very different from what the Fathers tell us."

"Different how?"

"Hush. Listen."

". . . so I told Mary. That's my friend. She lives next door to Reverend Parris. Those were the first children to have fits. His daughter, Betty, and Abigail Williams, a cousin. So I told my friend Mary that she simply had to get somebody to make a cake. You know. A cake. And feed it to the dog." Vaca Imunda looked around at the crew. "You know what I mean about a cake, right?"

They made no response.

"Everybody knows about witch cakes. Well. Maybe it's just certain people have been gifted with this knowledge." She dabbed her lips once more with her embroidered handkerchief and laid that hand, still clutching it, on the table. She took a deep breath. "First you get the urine from the children—"

The laugh coming from several of the crew was cut short by the lightning coming from Vaca Imunda's eyes.

"First you get the urine from the children. Then you bake it into a cake. Feed the cake to the dog. When the dog bites into the cake, the witch who caused the children's fits will cry out. It's very simple."

"Simple, all right," said Little Cock almost giving us away by his laughter.

"Stop. Don't get me laughing."

"Listen."

"It was her. It was Tituba. And she affected the others. She was the leader. And I can't talk with all you people mumbling in the corners like that. If I raise my voice, I might injure it."

"God forbid," said Tommy quietly, changing elbows at the rail. He tipped his head to make a further comment to Little Cock. "Tongue to the ass like a Jew's harp, that one, eh Pierce?"

Bosselé asked, "So I take it she was the first to be hanged then?"

"He's testing her," Little Cock said.

"Testing her? Why?"

"Hush."

"She wasn't hanged. She was jailed," said Vaca Imunda.

Lars spoke up then, egging her on, trying as well to get her to slip up on something. "This Tituba woman was the ringleader and they merely jailed her and hanged the rest?"

"She confessed her guilt. As the others should have done. Silly folks those people. I most certainly would have confessed my guilt right away rather than have it flogged out of me. But then again, I'm honest. And, of course, I would not ever have done any of those dreadful things in the first place, would I?" A dabbing of cheeks and chin with her embroidered handkerchief again.

I looked at Little Cock for an answer. Confess and stay alive? Deny and hang? This made no sense. Before he could explain this to me, I felt someone move in between and behind us. It was Jenny.

"What's going on?" she asked.

Little Cock reached back with one arm to draw Jenny in between us. "I believe your friend Vaca Imunda there is telling us your story."

"I'm innocent," she said. "I did nothing of that."

"I know," he said. "I know," and he squeezed her shoulder. "All the more reason now to find your daughter and get her away from wherever she is."

"After she got out of prison," Vaca Imunda continued, "Parris sold her—without her so-called 'husband'—to a fellow in Boston. Husband. Ha. It's only through the kindness of us Christians that we allow these people to pretend to marry. I can't possibly imagine God approving of 'marriage' between these… these creatures. I mean, they're… they're basically just animals, aren't they? Animals who can talk." Vaca Imunda leaned ahead onto her elbows and lowered her voice. "I heard this Boston fellow, this new owner, made 'advances' and beat her for refusing him. Silly girl. Serves her right for being so beautiful. Beautiful women deserve pain, don't you think? She had a baby with this, this 'husband' of hers, John Indian they called him. The child, a girl, would be around four years old now, I believe. The Reverend kept it. It would be the sister to the one he made with her." Something in this seemed particularly funny to Vaca Imunda and she screeched with laughter. "The Reverend Samuel Parris. Superior to all of us because of his knowledge of God. Supposed knowledge of God." She laughed again. "And there he was mixing with the animals and at the same time, from God's pulpit, telling *us* not to adulterate ourselves." Her laugh came so honestly and from such a deep place inside her, that she made us and the crew laugh along with her.

"She escaped from the Boston fellow in a dugout. I heard she was drowned at sea." Vaca Imunda's laughter at this made a squirrel run up the back of my neck.

Little Cock turned to Jenny. "You have two daughters. Two. Not one.

Two! When, pray tell, were you going to let me in on this piece of information?"

Jenny's eyes met his. "I thought it best to first let you know about one. Are you angry?"

"Furious. But I understand." Little Cock wrapped both arms around her and kissed her forehead. Then he pushed her away. "Wait. Husband. That woman spoke of a husband."

"John escaped from Samuel Parris. He found me in Boston. You were all correct. I could not possibly have handled that dugout by myself. We were headed for Salem to get my daughters, not knowing that my younger girl, Violet, was already in Boston. Sent away by Samuel Parris. And that Samuel Parris had sent off my older daughter, too—*his* daughter—to his plantation in Barbados. John and I tried but were blown off course during a gale. John lashed me in with his shirt. But before he could lash himself in, he was swept over. It was only through the grace of God that I remained alive and you found me."

"Who's that yammering over there behind those ropes?" demanded Vaca Imunda. "Show yourselves."

Everything happened so fast I can't accurately describe what the individual events were. I know that Jenny stepped out into the center of the deck first. This sent Vaca Imunda into a state that I had never before witnessed nor have since. There were a lot of words and phrases coming out of her mouth about the devil and curses and damnation and burning forever in the bowels of Hell. She shot to her feet and her chair went flying behind her into the shins of Cabin Boy who was standing behind her, arms crossed over his chest. While she flailed around on the deck, knocking the neat piles of rope askew, Cabin Boy cursed her then grabbed at her hair but caught only her bonnet. This sent her screams even higher. I'm sure the highest-flying eagle could hear them.

Then Vaca Imunda and Jenny were wrestling with each other on the deck. Vaca Imunda struggled to her feet to kick Jenny in the face but Jenny managed to catch Vaca Imunda's ankle and thus prevent anything more than a scrape to her face. Vaca Imunda landed on her bottom and the ship actually shuddered. Behind her, crew were recoiling the ropes she had tangled in her rage.

Little Cock was in there at some point trying to separate the women but got himself a strong blow to the nose for it. His nose didn't break but he looked like an amaljugwej, a raccoon, for several days afterwards.

The next thing I know, Vaca Imunda, who was not much taller but broader than Jenny, picked Jenny up and carried her, struggling like a mtesgm, a snake, toward the rail. Even though I knew he was in quite a lot of pain and his eyes were watering something awful, Little Cock ran to help but was no match for Vaca Imunda. She pushed him away so hard against the rail, I thought surely one of his ribs would have cracked.

Vaca Imunda wrapped her huge arm around Jenny's neck and while Jenny scraped and tore at the big woman's arm with her nails, Vaca Imunda managed to swing Jenny's legs up onto the rail. Jenny kicked and pushed against the rail but she was no match for the bigger woman. She was going over.

Captain KrommeZee stepped up behind the struggling women and with a belaying pin struck Vaca Imunda on the head so hard, the pin broke. She dropped to the deck. Bosselé and Little Cock, together, brought Jenny, gasping, over to where I was standing.

"The rest of you," said Captain KrommeZee calmly, "toss that garbage overboard."

"Yes, Sir!" said the entire crew in unison and with more enthusiasm than I would have expected from men I had learned were generally kind and accepting. Five of them scurried over to hoist Vaca Imunda up onto the rail. Grunting, they slid her bulk over. I was surprised I didn't hear a splash.

"Him, too," he said, pointing at Honey-Sop who was passed out snoring on the makeshift table. "We want no one telling of this in future." Little Cock and Lars dragged Honey-Sop to the starboard side and over he went, too. Oblivious all the way down to the water. He made no sound going in either.

Bosselé was already scrubbing the blood from Vaca Imunda's head off the deck.

I glanced up at Monsieur St-Amand who was at the wheel. He was unmoving and his mouth was open. I waved my hand at him as though to waken him from his bad dream. A smile without happiness curled one corner of his mouth. His shoulders went up. Captain KrommeZee climbed the steps to take the wheel back from him and although I barely heard the words, they were spoken so kindly, I knew he was telling Monsieur St-Amand to take care of Jenny and Little Cock.

I went to the port side to look over the rail and back to where Vaca Imunda had gone into the water. The ship was moving fast, creating watery cushions alongside that turned into geese vees behind it. Bobbing in the ship-made waves with her bright red hair wet and her arm waving at me, she looked less like a woodpecker now. Her mouth was still going but with cries for help rather than actual complaints coming out of it. At first I thought the flash of black triangle beside her might have been her wing after all, but then a flash of white, a rolling cloud of red in the water told me it wasn't. Woodpecker or not, Vaca Imunda was no more.

Twenty

I was happy it was daylight when we were finally settled in and the plank was down at the Boston Harbor dock. So many things happened so fast and all at once that I would have missed most of it even though I would have been happy that some things hadn't happened at all. The dock below was filled with all manner of people. If they had been tiny, I could say it looked like an an anthill squirming with creatures going in every direction but each with a purpose. Horses and carriages were arriving and after being loaded with either people or packages—sometimes both—they left in a clatter of horse hooves on wooden dock. Some carriages dropped off people and packages, too.

On the bow side of us was a huge weathered old ship with three high masts. It was so big and salt-coated that I knew it had to be a sea-going vessel. The dock curved in slightly at that spot so I could see quite a bit of the deck of that ship. I had noticed earlier, while we were docking, that the three men and two women who had been on the dock now stood on its deck. The men wore hats, long coats with dozens of undone buttons along the closure, and frilly white cloths around their necks and at their wrists. The women, one with a bright yellow dress and the other in a birch-leaf green dress, carried large red bags. Because of the way each woman moved the arm holding this bag, I knew it was very heavy. And I couldn't imagine what could be underneath the skirts of their dresses that could make them stand out so wide.

Then up from the hold of that other ship came four of the saddest creatures I think I will ever see. Their skin was dark brown with a gray haze to it and their hair was short, black and impossibly curly, with bits of stuff in it that I couldn't recognize and didn't want to in the first place. Iron bracelets circled their wrists and ankles. Their own wrists were joined with one chain, but the bracelets on their ankles were not chained together but to the person's ankle beside them. Chained at the ankle, two by two! I could not imagine how difficult it must have been to climb up from the hold wearing all that metal. One of the crew unlocked all the ankle bracelets then handed these to his fellow before pocketing the key. The fellow went below with the chains. Key Man pushed the female toward the visitors. She staggered with weakness—I could easily tell she was in poor condition—but she managed to stay on her feet. The three males were guided toward the visitors, too. These poor creatures were unclothed. But no, they were not creatures. These were humans. A woman and three men. Men? Hardly men. They were perhaps thirteen winters old at most. I turned my face away out of respect for them and as I did so, I heard a voice ask "… for these fine, healthy young Negroes? Let's say we start at fifteen pounds for a male and twenty for the female." This made me turn back to look. One of the men from shore stepped forward and with what I thought might be a short whip folded over, he jabbed the tallest of the boys in the chest. Hard. The brown-skinned woman groaned. She would be of an age that might make her the boy's mother. A crew man behind her spoke sharply. Her gaze returned to her feet in an all-too-familiar gesture. Slaves. I was acting as one of them now. But only *acting*. I thought of Jenny. How strong she must have been to survive this degradation.

Once again the man with the short folded whip jabbed the same boy. The boy made no protest, no face, no reaction. "I'll give you fifteen for this one."

"Twenty," said the second visiting man who stepped up to grab hold of the boy's ear to peer inside it. He wasn't gentle about it, either. He wrenched at the other ear. "Open your mouth, boy."

The boy's eyes widened as he looked to the crew member who had led him up from the hold. The crew member opened his own mouth wide.

The boy imitated this and the second man peered inside.

From behind the second man's shoulder, Visitor One stared into the boy's mouth, too. "Twenty-five."

Yellow Dress stepped forward. "Two hundred pounds for all four of them. But for the love of Heaven put some clothing on them. The sea wind is chilly this day."

Key Man made a gesture to one of the others—a man with a long beard done up in braids—who scurried away toward the prow of their ship. I couldn't see what he might be doing or where he might have gone because there were piles and piles of boxes and barrels sitting on the dock and being added to from the hold in a steady stream of products coming that would soon be taken off the ship. Pictures on some of these told me they contained molasses. Perhaps sugar in others.

Green Dress, one hand holding the end of her scarf across her nose, held out her large red bag to Yellow Dress. They exchanged bags. Yellow Dress opened it and showed the contents to Key Man.

He poked into it, said "Sold," then hung it on his belt.

Visitor One flapped his hand at Yellow Dress, making the frills on his wrist wave. To the crew member he said: "How many more below?"

Key Man called down into the hold. Grinning wide, he told Visitor One. "It wasn't such a good trip from the Indies this time, sire. We had a full dozen to start but…"

"But what? Be quick with it, man. I don't have all day to stand on this filthy vessel risking pestilence. Bring up the other eight for me to have a look at. See if they'll suit my purposes."

"Three, sire. That would be bring up the other three."

Visitor One crossed his arms, waving his folded whip in one hand and tapping his toe on the opposite side. "Be quick with it then!"

Behind him, the other two visiting men were already descending the gangplank and the man who had been sent away for clothing had returned with a few rags and was attempting to help Yellow Dress and Green Dress clothe the four humans Yellow Dress had just purchased. Several impatient gestures and some words I couldn't hear from Yellow Dress brought Key Man over to unlock the wrist bracelets. This made dressing these poor people much easier although I could see that they were so weak, it was all they could do to stay on their feet let alone raise their arms to put them into the sleeves of those rags.

From below came a cry of pain and then a brown head with black curly hair appeared at the opening of the hold. It was a man and it seemed he was climbing up the ladder backwards trying to pull something up with him. He was. In his arms was what appeared to be a young man sleeping. The young man sleeping disappeared back down. Curly disappeared just as quickly, like a squirrel yanked into a fox's den. I heard a thump below, an angry word and another cry of pain. A woman's cry of pain. A familiar one that I didn't want to think about. Then a male voice: "For the love of God, Jerome. Give us the focking key to unlock the shackles of these poor buggers or we'll be stuck here all week! The female's not goin' anywheres. Don't worry 'bout that." A cruel laugh.

Key Man stepped to the hold and dropped down the key. He waited a moment then the key flew up and he caught it.

Curly's head appeared once more along with two pairs of unshackled brown hands helping up the young man sleeping. The sleeping man's wrist bracelets and chain were still on him as they were on Curly. I soon saw that these men's ankles were still joined by chains. Curly struggled out of the opening and lay there on the deck for a moment, the young man lying on top of him. The next person I saw was a woman who was having great difficulty getting up the ladder.

Key Man had said three were left. I saw Curly. Two sets of brown hands. The sleeping man. That made four. No. The sleeping man was not sleeping. He was dead. I shivered to think of what it must be like to be chained to a dead man who was now lying on top of you. Curly's concern seemed to be directed to respectful handling of this young man's corpse and nothing else. He rolled the dead man off him, stood up, then taking gentle hold of the young fellow's lower leg, pulled him free of the edge of the hold.

"What's this, then?" demanded Visitor One pointing at them. "There's a plague aboard?" His neck frill was suddenly in his hand over his mouth.

"Excuse me for my bluntness, sire. But can ye not count?" To the woman who was just now getting her feet on deck, he snarled: "Hurry up. You heard the man. We've not got all day."

"What's wrong with this one then if it isn't plague?" demanded Visitor One pointing at the body of the young man.

"Nothing. Just dead is all."

The three surviving slaves, including the woman, were now huddled on the deck with the dead young man lying at their feet. The woman was with child and by the manner in which she was bending over and holding her belly, I knew the child would come soon. The third slave was gray haired and even thinner than the dead young man.

"Hurry, hurry. Come stand here, you lazy lot."

They shuffled toward Visitor One, the old man holding the woman's elbow, her face twisted in agony as she leaned against him and tried, I knew, to hold back any sound. They were not chained in any way. Curly bent over again to drag his partner across the deck.

Key Man shrugged at Visitor One. "If only this one had lasted one more night in the hold he would have brought me at least thirty pounds.

He's young. Now he'll just be stinking up our air until we're far enough at sea to toss him to the sharks. Mustn't bring those nasty teeth into your nice harbor by tossing him too close to shore, must we?" His giggle made me shiver.

Now below on the busy dock, Yellow Dress and Green Dress stood with their newly acquired property. The way the sun struck the face of Green Dress just as I glanced over told me that she was not entirely White. Her cheekbones were high and flat and the color of her skin was warm. Was she a slave also then? The demeanor between these two women hadn't given me any indication that they were mistress and slave.

Because I was a healer, my ears were attuned to screams of any kind so when I heard a high-pitched cry coming from somewhere behind us, my hand reached out to grasp Monsieur St-Amand's arm. "What's that?"

"Cart wheels. The ship aft." Then in a whisper. "Better move your hand away."

"Oh. Sorry." I tried not to smile. "Master." I folded my hands against my waist.

From the ship aft, men were unloading boxes and boxes piled high with fish. At the bottom of their gangplank, other men met them with side-less carts which they loaded with fish then rolled, wheels squeaking and squealing, over to several long tables. Men and women stood behind these tables, their arms and hands moving so fast they were blurred. Fish guts flowed over the front edge of the tables into even more boxes. The gutted fish were tossed behind the men and women into more boxes sitting on more tables. Workers took these away to load onto large wagons some of which were pulled by as many as four horses. Other workers removed the guts to carts and hurried away with them.

I was at the rail but still, the smell of fish was so strong, it made me sneeze. At my side, Monsieur St-Amand—Master Gooden—asked: "Are you quite all right?"

Another sneeze. "Yes." Another. "Fish. One at a time for me please. I've never seen—or smelled—so many."

"They're off to be salted. It's a valuable trade." Monsieur St-Amand flipped a handkerchief over my clasped hands. I could see the letters EG, raised and shining with silk thread, on the near corner of it. Monsieur was well-prepared for subterfuge, too, it seemed.

"Thank you, Master." As I wiped my nose with the embroidered handkerchief of my slave master Edward Gooden, I laughed.

"What now?"

"Aren't I turning into the proper English lady? Slave or not? Master."

"Indeed you are. Look." Monsieur St-Amand leaned his head close to mine and stretched his arm out at my eye level toward the horizon. "See it? The carriage?"

In the distance, I could see two horses pulling what looked like a big dark brown box with a figure sitting on it but not much more. "Who is it?"

"That will be my… my friend… coming to pick us up. Where's Pierce?"

As though in a rehearsed move, we turned our heads in opposite directions to search the deck. Pierce— Little Cock—was standing near the helm with Bosselé. Their heads were close together as they spoke, lips barely moving.

"He's there," I said. "What's he up to?"

"He's staying behind for now. You and I and Jenny will be going with my friend. His name is James Hunter. That's all you need to know about him. At least for the moment."

Another squeal from a cart—this time accompanied by shouts from the two men handling it—caused me to look toward the area where Yellow Dress and Green Dress had been tending to their charges. Yellow Dress was no longer there but the red bag of coins was still on Green Dress's arm. Behind Green Dress, a wheeled fish cart—this one with sides—had tipped over, spilling fish and parcels wrapped in heavy sailcloth across the yard. I didn't need to be a soldier to see that many of these wrapped parcels were muskets. Some had to be pistols. The boxes no doubt held shot and gunpowder.

"What—?"

The men quickly righted the cart and began to place the several parcels back into it.

"Say nothing." Monsieur St-Amand placed his arm across the front of my body. "Just pray silently."

Green Dress said something to the four slaves with her and they all stepped to the scattering of fish and firearms to block it from the view of the slave ship and the anthill of workers and passersby as best they could. Green Dress's full skirt did a perfect job of floating like a wikuom over most of the wrapped packages. From an alleyway about six buildings away came several people: men, women and even a little girl, all brown skinned. I counted eight. The little girl crawled under Green Dress's skirt to first retrieve what was probably a pistol and a bag of gunpowder, then a few other items. Within the time it takes four crows to pass a message to one another and back again, all the packages were in the cart. With everyone helping, the fish went on top and the cart was rolled away. Everyone except Green Dress disappeared calmly behind the building.

There was so much going on that I almost missed seeing Bosselé and Little Cock standing together now on the dock at the bottom of our gangplank. There, Bosselé took hold of Little Cock's shoulders and adjusted his body so he would be facing the alleyway the people had come out of. Although they spoke softly, I could hear their words: "See the sign with the pig just short of a hundred yards yonder?"

"I do."

"That's the Blind Pig Inn. Go to the rear door and ask for Gracie Waite."

A long handshake and a warm embrace and Little Cock ran off. When Bosselé reached the top of the gangplank on his return to the deck of our ship, he passed a look to Monsieur St-Amand. I was not able to read the thoughts that went from one mind to the other. I only knew the most dangerous part of our journey was about to start.

Twenty-one

Over at the slave ship, the crew had completed unloading their barrels and boxes and men were now hauling barrels and boxes aboard. Visitor One was still there. The woman was doubled over in labor and the old gray-haired man was trying to keep her upright as best he could. I imagine it was Key Man who had removed the shackles from Curly and the dead man because the dead man now lay on top of several boxes near the rail and some men were covering him with sail cloth.

Visitor One waved his folded whip at the woman and the old man. "I most certainly am not the least bit interested in these two. But this one …" He poked his whip into Curly's stomach.

Curly did not react.

"Thirty pounds, you say? Very well." Visitor One fished into a pouch on his belt and began to count out coins. With his head bent, and with Key Man looking down to keep track of the coin count, neither of them noticed that Curly had shuffled slightly away. Curly moved his right leg back. I knew what he was about to do and prayed he would have the strength for it. Like a summer aplíkmuj, a brown hare, he shot to the gangplank and down it into the crowd below.

Visitor One dropped his whip, reached back inside his multi-unbuttoned coat and pulled out a pistol. He cocked it, aimed it, fired.

From within the crowd came two cries. First, one from a child and next, no doubt, from the child's mother.

Curly kept running.

Green Dress pointed to the Blind Pig Inn and said something as Curly ran past her.

Visitor One reached around to the other side of his belt and pulled out a second pistol. Cocked it, aimed it, fired.

Curly went down.

"Merde!" came out of my mouth just as a dockworker passed by me with a cluster of hams hanging over his shoulder.

He stopped walking and showed me the inside of his mouth. "What did you say?"

Lars and Woodpecker Food who were working near us to direct the loading of wares, both turned to look at me, frightened looks on their faces. Monsieur St-Amand said nothing but I heard a small gasp and saw his hands almost become fists.

I dabbed my mouth with Monsieur St-Amand's silk handkerchief and coughed into it. "My, my. I cannot abide the stench of fish."

Ham Fellow closed his mouth and moved on.

"My, my." I coughed again at his back. "Positively dreadful, eh what?"

From beside me, Monsieur St-Amand growled. "That's quite enough, *Dawn!* Don't overdo it."

I bent my knees in a quick curtsey. "Yes, Master Gooden."

Where Curly had gone down I saw that the same group from the alleyway had assembled around him. A woman was on her knees, tending to him. The little girl, carrying a bottle in one hand and with long strips of cloth flying behind her from the other, arrived breathless and handed the bottle to the kneeling woman. He was still alive, then. Good.

A commotion from the slave ship took my eyes away so I didn't see the group from the alleyway lift Curly up and carry him off.

Visitor One had retrieved his whip after dropping it to the deck and was now beating Key Man across the head with it still folded.

Key Man's head was down, his arms were folded across his head. "You paid for 'im. *Ow.* That resolves me of all responsibility. *Ow.* Have ye no honor, sire?"

Brandishing a huge knife, the crewman who had collected the clothes for the four slaves, the one with the long braided beard, came running in. "Ye dirty bastard." He made the Sign of the Cross in the air with his knife, not on himself but like a Father would at the end of his Mass. "I'll not think twice of removing your innards with my trusty blade, sire. We've already one to throw to the sharks. I'm certain they'd appreciate yet another. One with more meat on 'im. Get ye off our ship."

Visitor One was not easily put off, I'll give him that. "I want my money back. A runner's of no value to me and a dead one's less." Nose high, smile smug, he swung around to indicate, with a sweep of whip, his dead purchase laying on the ground—the purchase he himself had shot—but like Ham Fellow, his mouth dropped open, too. "Where did he go?" He twirled again and raised his whip to strike Key Man. "You filthy cheats. This was a trick to take my money."

Suddenly, from behind Visitor One, a swarthy crewman with a missing eye and dressed in red from headscarf to boots threw one arm around his neck and restrained the wrist holding the whip with the other. Braided Beard closed in with the edge of his knife against Visitor One's throat just below where One Eye's arm was. "Can ye feel the touch of my blade?"

As best he could with an arm below his chin, Visitor One nodded.

"If I had a mind to shave in the first place, I could do it with this blade o' mine, it's that honed. I suggest ye go, sire. The dead slave—dead or not and I doubt the former—is yours. I suggest you go find him down that alley by The Blind Pig. If ye dare, that is."

Visitor One relaxed against the man behind him and opened his hand to release his whip once more.

Braided Beard slipped his knife into his belt. "But I must warn ye if ye don't have the brains to already know: that's not the best alleyway to go into if you have even the slightest smell of wealth about you. Even in the daylight."

With his arm still around Visitor One's neck, One Eye brought him to the top of the gangplank. He held him there.

Bearded Braid said: "Looks like ye're being given a choice, sire. He wants to know if ye'll be walkin' down the plank on your own or if ye wants him to throw ye."

Visitor One croaked *walk* and the big man set him down.

Twenty-two

The crowd parted and Monsieur St-Amand's friend, James Hunter, handling a big fancy carriage with room inside for six came thundering into the ship yard. People scattered. Some men removed their hats and bowed; some women curtsied.

"How did he know we'd be here this exact morning at this exact time?" I asked Monsieur St-Amand. "It's not like the weather allows a schedule."

"You didn't see them then?"

"See who?"

"For one, the pigeon I picked up in Salem. And the others I brought along."

"You and your pigeons. You've had them on board the whole time? Where did you hide them?"

With a glint in his eye, he smiled over at me. "Come now, my dear Dawn, we have to have *some* secrets between us, do we not?"

I was beginning to realize we had a lot more than "some" secrets between us. I didn't know this man as well as I thought I had. This made me uncomfortable.

As the carriage neared the dock it was stopped by a man waving his arms and yelling. A knot of women had clustered around something on the ground.

The child! The child I had heard cry out when Visitor One fired his first pistol.

The carriage stopped and Master Hunter beckoned us to hurry.

"Where's Jenny?" I asked. "She should be up on deck by—"

"Right behind you." Bosselé, arms laden with most of our luggage, indicated a figure beside him. The figure was completely veiled. Gloves covered her hands. She carried two small bags one of which she handed to me. It was my munti.

I leaned in close. "Is that you, Jenny?"

A nod and a giggle confirmed it was.

"Let's go then."

At last we would be safely on shore. Or so I thought.

***

In single file, Monsieur St-Amand, me, Bosselé, then Jenny descended the gangplank. I took a few steps. My feet were not expecting to feel what they felt so I staggered slightly. Little Cock had told us about "sea legs." I now knew for certain what he meant. I stopped walking for three breaths. Laughed. Then followed Monsieur St-Amand across the dock toward his friend's carriage.

His friend waited beside the left hand horse, his hand under its chin as it bobbed its head up and down. Master Hunter was about Monsieur St-Amand's height but he was wider in the shoulders and had a bigger belly. He wore a white shirt with ruffles at the neck and a wide smooth collar that went half way up to his chin, a vest the color of the inside of a clamshell, a short jacket over it in a darker shade of clamshell from which the frilly sleeves of his shirt protruded, black shoes with gold buckles and white stockings that went up to his knees. His hat was black and trimmed with delicate gold swirls along its edges; the front of it curled inward on both sides of a gap. He was quite a handsome man and looked to be very wealthy from what I had l learned from my experiences with Newcomers back home. My people did not have to provide a dowry to get one of our men to marry one of our women, but I knew what a dowry was. I think the dowry for Monsieur St-Amand's new bride would be a big one. I would ask him later if she was the only heir to Master Hunter's fortune.

As we passed by the group huddling around the child, I couldn't help myself, I looked over. From this new viewpoint, I could see that it was a boy around J-B's age, ten winters. He was bleeding from the inner thigh.

"We have to help him," I said. "He's going to die if we don't." I stepped away from our group and approached the people. One of them saw me coming and motioned that the others step back from the child. They did.

When I got to him, I went down onto my knees and opened my munti. But as I reached in to get my eagle feather, Monsieur St-Amand came up beside me and grabbed both my wrists.

"For the love of God don't touch him!"

As I looked up at Monsieur St-Amand, I could see the faces of the people around him. Their eyes were wide and I could see the gold in their teeth.

"But—"

He bent down as if trying to raise me to my feet but pressed his lips close to my ear. He whispered. "Not another word or they'll see you burned at the stake."

"Wha—?" I closed my mouth and allowed him to lift me to my feet, leaving my open munti on the ground. A woman dressed in a black shirt and grey skirt leaned over to look inside it. If it could be possible, her eyes got even bigger.

"Witch," she growled at me. "She's a—"

Before she could continue, Master Hunter, all smiles, had her by the arm and was leading her aside. I caught only part of what he said: "Martha.

One more word and your husband's contract with me will be terminated. Do you understand?"

"Yes, sire."

"Thank you. Now please explain to your friends here that my friend, Edward Gooden is greatly experienced in matters of doctoring. That his slave here, is merely his assistant. Do you understand?"

"Yes, sire."

The woman returned to the group. "They will do their best to save your boy's life, Ruthie. Master Hunter vouches for their good will."

As Monsieur St-Amand and I bent to our task, he said quietly. "Give me no instructions directly. I will pretend to be asking you what the next step is as though I am your teacher and am testing you."

I nodded.

"Above all," he continued. "Do not touch the boy and do not at all, bring out anything from your bag there. Agreed?"

"Agreed." I closed my munti. "Uh, Master."

Monsieur St-Amand spoke to the one named Ruthie. "May I have your permission to cut open the boy's pants leg? I must deal with his wound and the clothing hinders me."

"By all means, sire. Do what you must."

"I think it best, also, that you divert your—"

Just then, a woman behind Ruthie pointed away and cried out. "That's the bastard there! He's the one what shot 'im!"

The crowd, including Ruthie, rushed away crying out. "Get him. String him up. Murderer."

Master Hunter stepped in close to Monsieur St-Amand. "I'll take this opportunity when the rabble is otherwise occupied, to get my hat to your boy, Pierce. He's that skinny little fellow with the bright blue jacket. The one that came off the ship with Bosselé, is he not? Then took off toward the Blind Pig Inn?"

"The very one."

Monsieur St-Amand and I were alone. As quickly as possible, we tended to the boy's wound.

"His hat?"

"A signal for the man who comes to collect him later. That's all you need to know. This doesn't look as bad as I had feared. I think we can indeed save him. What's your name, boy?"

"Persistence," the young fellow whispered proudly.

Monsieur St-Amand and I looked at each other and together we said "Good name."

"We know someone brave and strong called Persistence. Pierce for short."

The boy cringed a few times while we tended to him but, bravely, he did not cry out.

When we were finished and putting everything away, he looked up at Monsieur St-Amand and said quietly. "You're one of them, aren't you? One of them what helps the Negroes."

"Say nothing of this, boy. Nothing." Master Hunter had come back.

"Of course not, sire. Although I love my mother, I do not agree with the policies that she and Father and their friends hold toward the free Negroes. I am on your side."

"What policies are those?" I asked, forgetting myself once again. I could see from my eye's corner that a larger crowd had gathered and four or five men were dragging Visitor One along the ground by a rope around his neck. "What are they doing to him? They'll choke him to death if they continue!"

"He's gonna hang anyway," said Persistence. "Nobody likes him in the first place. And he shot a child. Me." He smiled but the smile didn't last for long. "Perhaps it might be better if you ran over there to tell them I'm not dead?"

"I say there!" Master Hunter called out. One of the men turned. "The boy is fine. He'll be fine. Let Joseph go."

Another man called back. "Must we?"

Three of his fellows laughed.

The man who had called back turned to the others: "Let him go. Fate will eventually take care of him." He waved to Master Hunter. "Situation resolved, sire."

Master Hunter took Monsieur St-Amand by the arm. "Let's go. My horses are restless."

I looked to where the carriage was to see a young man doing his best to steady the head of that one horse. He was managing to keep the horse in one place, but not easily. Her face now unveiled, Jenny waved at me from inside the carriage.

Monsieur St-Amand: "You found Pierce? Has he made the acquaintance of Mistress Waite yet?"

"She's on an errand. Someone told him to stay in the alleyway until her return. As planned, I told him to be certain to wear that hat so my driver will know who he is to pick up at Willem's ship at midnight. He's dark skinned enough to be safe there, I think. I hope."

"Midnight. Yes. A good time. Many distractions going on. But how will—?"

Master Hunter pointed at a small pocket in his vest.

"Ah. You gave him your timepiece. Good."

As we climbed into Master Hunter's carriage, I noticed that most of the people who had been clustered around Persistence, then around Visitor One, were now clustered around us and pointing. Most of them frowning.

Master Hunter disappeared from my view onto the bench at the top of the carriage. Before we moved, I heard him say: "Be off with you now. Go about your business and forget everything you've seen if you know what's good for you. Be off."

Obediently, everyone scattered and we were propelled away on a bumpy journey to the home of Master James Hunter.

Twenty-three

It felt good to be swaying again. It was true what Little Cock had told us about spending many days on a ship. It made your head do strange things to your feet when they touched land again. I could feel myself falling asleep. At one time, I felt a thin blanket being placed over me and pulled up to my chin. My sleepy eyes opened to see that it was Monsieur St-Amand who was doing this. Jenny was already covered by a bright red blanket and was sound asleep. I didn't waken again until I felt the carriage speed up.

"Young horses," said Monsieur St-Amand. "The closer to home they get, the more enthusiastic they are. Don't forget your bag under the seat."

The one thing I would never forget was my munti. I bent to retrieve it and as I did, I glanced out the window of the carriage. We were approaching an enormous house painted white with green trim and a red door in the center of it. There were two windows on each side of the door; five windows on the next floor up; and five more windows with their own little rooves coming out of the main roof.

"Everyone from my village would fit in there."

"It's one of the biggest in the district. There are attached structures behind that go all the way to the treeline."

I said nothing about that but I wondered how large a family Master Hunter must have to need such a large house. I soon found out that his family was one daughter, no wife, but his house was full of servants of every skin color I could have imagined and who all seemed to be happy.

I was shown my room by a dark-skinned man who insisted on carrying even my munti up the high wooden stairs to the second floor. While I unpacked, a young woman of about fifteen winters brought in a meal for me. She placed the tray on a small table with two chairs over by the window, looked me straight in the eye and asked: "Anythin' else, mum?"

"Thank you. Everything is… Well. Everything is everything."

"I'm mor'n happy to hear that, mum."

I liked the way she talked. "You sing when you talk."

"It's me Irish heritage, mum."

"Are you…? Are you a slave here?"

"Heavens, no, mum. Indentured servant now but me time's almost up. When you're a servant for James Hunter, your time goes faster. He—" Her eyes went to the floor then back up at me. "I shouldn't be tellin' you about my boss's business, should I?"

She stepped into the hall, stopped, turned, then came back to stand beside the bed. "A'most forgot, mum." She pointed to a metal knob hanging from a fine chain that came out of the wall. "If there's anything you might be needin', give that a pull. Someone'll come to do your bidding." A curtsy, a smile, and she was gone.

The bed looked comfortable so I ate my meal as quickly as possible and slipped under the covers where it seemed that I had slept for only a moment when I felt hands on me as someone—Jenny—was shaking me awake. There was no light coming in through the curtains so I knew it had to be the middle of the night. I had slept for a lot longer than I thought.

"Come with me," she said, her eyes wide. "Pierce has been hurt. Master Gooden wants you."

I slipped into a thick housecoat and followed her down the hall to what was now Little Cock's room. He was lying on the bed on top of the covers while Master Hunter and Monsieur St-Amand leaned over him. On the side table sat a dish of water with blood-stained cloths in it. A large white bandage was wrapped around Little Cock's head. His left eye was swollen almost shut. The men were wrapping wide bandages around his ribcage.

"What happened?" I asked thinking of both Honey-Sop and Jacques l'Itale when I saw the head bandage. "Are you all right?"

"I am now," said Little Cock. "Ow."

"Sorry," said Master Hunter. "Too tight?"

"No. It was me. I anticipated." A nervous laugh.

"What happened?" I asked again as the same young woman who'd brought my evening meal entered the room with a tray of steaming mugs. It smelled like coffee. "I thought you didn't drink coffee in New England."

"Some don't. I'm not one of them," said Master Hunter.

"Will you be needin' anything further?" asked the young woman. "Any of you?"

Master Hunter raised his eyebrows first at Monsieur St-Amand, at Jenny, then at me. We all shook our heads *no*.

"That'll be all, Aideen. Thank you."

"It won't be too long till dawn. Shall I alert Missus Cleary to start breakfast for—" she glanced at me. "Is it all right to talk openly in front of these people?"

"It is, Aideen. And yes. Please waken Missus Cleary. We'll need not only the mid-morning meal but ten will be shipping out before sunset so we'll need stores enough for… What say, Edward? Three weeks?"

"That should be plenty. Willem KrommeZee has enough stores aboard to last for a trip to the Gold Coast and back again. Twice." He laughed. "I've never seen a man better prepared for every eventuality."

"It's a good way to be when conducting this nasty business." He turned to Little Cock. "What got you beaten? We must know. Leave out no detail. Lives depend on it."

Little Cock's eyes sought mine for a moment. I knew nothing more than he did so I shrugged.

"Why did they beat you?"

"They stole my gold."

"I never thought of it," said Monsieur St-Amand, his hand seeking his forehead. "In that section of town, it would have been best if you'd given it all to me for safe keeping. I'm very sorry you've lost it all."

"Oh. But I got it back."

"You did? How?"

"I returned the favor." Little Cock's smile was sly.

We all looked at each other.

"Don't forget. I was trained by pirates. I'm small but I fight like a demon."

I sat on one side of the bed. Jenny sat on the other side. Master Hunter and Monsieur St-Amand chose chairs which they pulled up close.

"Two of them. They bashed in my head. When I awoke, I bashed in theirs. One of them for good, I'm afraid."

Monsieur St-Amand crossed his arms and leaned back in his chair. His mouth was tight.

"I was waiting outside the inn for this woman called Gracie Waite to return from her errands." To Master Hunter he said, "Bosselé. He's one of the crew. I knew him from… from before."

"I know who Bosselé is. Continue."

One of Little Cock's eyebrows went up at me. "Bosselé told me I could get information about my sister. Her name is Lilac. From this woman. So I waited there. And I waited fully knowing what was going on inside that building." He glanced at me. "Rum."

I reached out to take his hand in both of mine. "You did it, though. I mean you didn't. You stayed strong."

"I did. But it cost me dearly."

"Your money?"

"But you said you got it all back," said Jenny.

"I did. But now there's a price on my head."

Monsieur St-Amand spoke. "For?"

"For killing a man."

"Self-defense, you said. "They can't hold you responsible when you were attacked yourself."

"I didn't say self-defense. It was revenge. They knocked me out. When I came to, one of them was outside in the alley being serviced by a doxie. There was a wooden box there. Broken. I took a board from it and caved the bastard's head in. The doxie screamed. The other fellow came running out. I bashed his head in, too. The doxie screamed some more. I ran."

"But… You said they accused you. Did someone follow you?"

"I headed for the docks. Back to the ship. Back to where I was supposed to be picked up." He drifted off into a memory for a moment. "So many thieves and doxies along the way. Out there at the docks. Where I used to travel with impunity because… because I was one of them…"

I squeezed his hand. "Don't go there. Finish the story. Why did you go back?"

"I forgot the damned hat. The one I was to wear so Master Hunter's driver would recognize me and bring me here. I had to go back."

"And that's when the crowd saw you?" asked Monsieur St-Amand.

"The hat was full of blood from my head wound. Didn't take many brains to match the pattern. I thought I was done for."

"You must have been terrified," I offered.

"I was, but as luck would have it, the carriage went by and Roger,

Master Hunter's driver, being a curious and nosy sort, slowed the horse down. One of the ladies—ladies? hah!—was trying to take the hat from me and as I was holding it high in the air to prevent this from happening, Roger took it as a signal. He came to my rescue."

"Roger is a valuable friend," Master Hunter said.

"What's more than good is the respect your name has in this town," Little Cock told him. "The crowd recognized him immediately and dispersed."

"Let's leave Pierce alone to get some rest now, shall we?" Master Hunter rose from his chair. "We have a full day scheduled for tomorrow." To me, Jenny, and Little Cock he said, "There is much you are unaware of. I'll explain more at breakfast."

"Gracie Waite was in the crowd," Little Cock said. "I knew exactly who she had to be the moment I laid eyes on her."

"You found your sister?" I was delighted.

"Not my Lilac. Gracie Waite looks so much like her. And the age would be right. Although she might be too old. I don't know."

Master Hunter stopped at the door with his hand on the knob and his back to us. "She is Lilac's daughter."

"Where is my sister then? She's all right? She lives here in Boston?"

Master Hunter still did not turn around but shook his head. "She didn't make it. She died in childbirth. She was only thirteen years old after all."

"That bastard!"

Master Hunter opened the door and stepped into the hall. "Pierce needs to rest up. We have much to do tomorrow." From the small pocket of his vest he removed a gold watch. "Make that today."

"What's going on?" I called out as he walked away down the hall. I went to the door to follow him but Monsieur St-Amand took my arm. Behind him, Jenny was helping Little Cock get under the covers.

"I'm too angry to sleep," Little Cock said.

"Sleep anyway." She pulled the thick blanket up to his chin and tucked it behind his shoulders. "You want to look your best to meet your niece. *Si?*" She patted his cheek. "Sleep."

To me, Monsieur St-Amand said: "At daybreak you and I will take the carriage to the Blind Pig Inn where we will meet with Gracie Waite. *And* Captain KrommeZee. *And* others. You will finally understand what I do with my life, and my pigeons." He smiled. "When I'm not acting as a surgeon at the fort in Port Royal. And furthermore, why I must stay here."

My mouth opened but before a question could come out of it, he put his finger to my lips.

"How is your patience level? Can you wait? It will be much easier to show you than to tell you."

I spun around. "I'm going back to bed. Wake me when it's time to leave." I didn't think I would be able to sleep but I would try. I had a feeling the next few days were going to be demanding all my strength.

Twenty-four

As I drifted off to sleep under the warm soft blankets of Hunter Manor, I thought I might like to talk with Falcon about moving away from our village, and the wikuom we shared with each other and our children, into a house. A house with a bedroom and mattresses and pillows just like these. Above all, pillows. Just like these… But once again it seemed like my back had only just sunk into the feather mattress when a soft knock at the door made me sit up.

It was Aideen. "I have breakfast for you, mum. Pancakes with maple syrup from your area of the world, no less. How do you like that?" She set the tray down on the little table by the window, pointed with one finger to each object on the plate: "Sausage and biscuits. Coffee, of course. Loads of it. Shall I pour you a mug of it, mum?"

I wasn't sure of my surroundings just yet. I swung my legs out from under the blankets and fluffed my hair. "Did I sleep at all?"

"You did, mum." She pointed to my feet. "The chamber pot's under there."

I used it.

"I'll be helpin' you dress while you eat, mum. So sorry, but your Master Gooden is in a hurry to get going and Roger has the carriage ready."

Help me dress? I was beginning to realize why the women in this area of the world appeared to be so helpless. "I think I can manag—"

Three thumps at the door and Monsieur St-Amand's voice. "What's keeping you so long? We're ready to go."

Aideen's face and her upturned hands and raised shoulders told me her unspoken words: *Told you so.*

I let her help me dress. She was right, it was much faster this way. I chewed on sausage—it was good—while she buttoned me up where I needed to be buttoned up.

"I'll just wrap the rest of that up for you, mum, so you can take it with you. I'll meet you out front at the carriage. Be off with you before he gets any more impatient."

***

I draped my skirts over one arm as I rushed down the stairs. I made sure to hold the handrail with the other as I wasn't used to these shoes of mine, even yet. I didn't think I would ever be. At the bottom of the stairs I caught a glimpse of a woman around my age. She was passing through the doorway into the dining room where we had conducted our meeting. Marguerite had taught me well: I knew this woman's dress was made of silk. It was as blue as a moonless night sky. A white lace ruff below her chin made her skin look even paler than I could imagine a woman's skin could ever be. A cloud of the most unbearable sadness drifted up to me. A phrase I had learned from reading those extremely sad French novels about love, and especially loss, that Geneviève had taught me to read when I was a young girl came to mind: "Elle était résigné à son terrible sort, she was resigned to her terrible fate."

And what fate would that be?

She must have seen me from the corner of her eye because she came back out of the dining room to meet me at the bottom of the stairs. "You must be Edward's friend. Dawn, is it?"

"It is."

She was even sadder up close. A tiny little thing. With her hands clasped at her waist she resembled someone expecting a thrashing.

"And you are?"

"Marie."

"I take it you are the…" My brain searched for the right term. "… the lady of the house?"

"I am."

"The fiancée of my friend Mons— uh, Master Gooden."

"Yes. Edward. My father's dear friend for many years and I've known Edward almost as long."

"So you love him then."

"I love no other."

"You love only Master Gooden then?" I was fishing without thread or hook. I needed to know if there was love between my good friend and this sad, emaciated, empty woman.

"I love no other."

The front door into the foyer banged open and Monsieur St-Amand stood there. He was dressed in a long unbuttoned coat, frilly neck piece and sleeves, similar to what Visitor One and Visitor Two had been wearing on the slave ship the day before. "Let's go," he said to me and without a glance at Marie.

I stepped forward and he pushed me onto the veranda. "Get in the carriage." In the same tone he called out behind me into the room, "I expect we shall share a meal alone together after I return, my darling, my love. You know, to make arrangements for the wedding."

In that voice he calls her darling and love?

"I will be wanting fowl."

Her quiet obedient voice responded: "Yes, Edward. I'll see to it."

"Not for my evening meal, my love. For the wedding dinner. It will be venison tonight. Tell them not to forget the onion rub. I dislike the wild taste of deer without the onion rub."

"Yes, Edward. I'll see to it. Safe journey."

"Of course." Then back to me. "Get inside the carriage. Now. Go."

Little Cock, who was sitting up on top of the carriage beside a man wearing a billowing white shirt, a blue vest and light brown pants, looked down at me and made a face as if to say "What has happened to Monsieur St-Amand?" Little Cock wore a similar billowing shirt but in pale blue.

I hoped my face told Little Cock that I didn't know any more than he did about it.

Monsieur St-Amand boosted me up into the carriage. With one leg on the step he grasped the bar beside the door and called up. "Let's go, Roger."

He sat on the bench beside me.

***

Along the way I learned that James Hunter, good and long-time friend of Monsieur St-Amand who would "now and always and henceforth" (there were those big legal words again) be known as Edward Gooden, was dying.

"Is that why Marie is so sad? Because her father is dying?"

"Sad? She's not sad. She's like that all the time. She's just… Just Marie. That's all." His expression did not change.

"Is that why you're so sad?"

The look he gave me, if I had been anybody else but me, would have made me shrink up like an oak leaf in autumn.

"And you're going to be happy with this woman for the rest of your life? What joy will there be in your relationship?"

"None of this is any of your business, Dawn. She and I will benefit from our association with each other. I know her well. What more does one need?"

I felt sorry for both Monsieur St-Amand and his bride-to-be but decided to keep this to myself to avoid further burning looks from Monsieur St-Amand. "What's wrong with Master Hunter?"

"Something internal. Incurable. Inevitable."

We arrived at the Blind Pig Inn. The horses jerked to a stop and the driver leaped down to open the carriage door on Monsieur St-Amand's side. Little Cock climbed down on my side. He was looking much better than he had last night. A large floppy hat covered his head bandage. He opened the door on my side, bowed low and held out one hand, palm side up for me to take.

I tried not to laugh at his twisted up body as I took his hand.

I descended from the carriage. "Thank you."

"Nuttin' but a pleasure for me, mum."

My laugh burst out. He tried to keep his inside but wasn't able.

On the other side of the carriage I heard: "Thank you, Roger. Come along, Dawn. Hurry, hurry. I must introduce you to Gracie Waite, the mistress of the inn."

I came around to his side where he leaned close to my ear. "I will tell you three things. One: The reason for our being here. Two…" (this one through his teeth): "Maintain your decorum. Control your words, and your laughter especially. Three: Don't ever pry into my private life again. Stay out of my head."

He went first through the door into the inn.

To his back I said: "Or what?"

Twenty-five

I stepped inside the Blind Pig Inn. This was a huge room with many wide beams running across the ceiling along their narrow edges. Other beams held these up. Under my feet, wide smooth planks made up the floor. The walls, though. The walls were entirely covered with pictures. I turned to touch a picture beside the entrance door to learn that the pictures hadn't been drawn directly onto the walls, but that the walls had been covered with special paper with the pictures already on it. It was beautiful. I had seen pictures on the pages of books but these pages were much, much larger than any I could have imagined. The deep turquoise swirls at the edges of the walls matched not only the paint on the columns, but also the cupboards against the far wall.

A woman in a red shirt and skirt and wearing a tight-fitting white bonnet ran up to Monsieur St-Amand and threw her arms around him. They kissed each other's cheeks, both sides, then their lips touched briefly, too.

She was shorter than I was but not by a lot, and the hair I could see under her bonnet was dark, dark brown. She was rather pretty with dusky skin and the features of our people. She pointed at Little Cock with her chin. "Is this he?"

"Indeed it is," said Monsieur St-Amand, smiling for the first time that morning.

"You look so much like her," said Little Cock reaching out to take her into his arms. "I'm your uncle."

"Uncle Pierce," interjected Monsieur St-Amand. "Uncle Pierce." He glanced over at me then turned away so I wouldn't see the wetness in his eyes, but I did. "All right then. Enough of this. We have work to do. Lots of it and dangerous work. What can you tell us, Gracie?"

Grasping her newly met uncle's hand, she motioned us to a back room where six or seven men and women, all in long white gowns and tight white hats, worked preparing food. We passed through this room to another doorway without anyone giving us more than the corner of an eye. We entered yet another room, this one with wooden boxes and barrels piled high making a canyon through it. Behind this room, another, windowless and full of chairs and tables stacked on top of each other, an old sink. Gracie led us to the far corner of this room where she leaned down, still holding onto Little Cock's hand, to push a section of the wall near the floor. I heard a click and a slit appeared in the wall. It was a panel. Gracie slid this open and motioned us to follow her into a long narrow corridor.

At the end of this corridor another led off to the right which would lead back into the main inn. Gracie did not turn down this corridor but instead, pointed with the thumb of her free hand. "In case someone makes it this far, they'll think that's the right way to go." Up high in the left hand corner, she pushed another section of wood and the hidden door in front of us exposed its secret.

She called out: "By the grace of God."

A woman's voice answered: "We are saved."

We followed Gracie into a large, windowless room lit with one lamp. A fireplace at the far corner of the room was not lit. It didn't even have ashes or wood in it. I didn't think it had ever been used. She released Little Cock's hand.

I looked over at his face. I don't think he had taken his eyes off her since they had embraced in the inn's entrance room. He seemed entirely at peace. His back was straight, his chin was held high. He was taller than I'd thought.

Gracie turned to me. "Dawn, is it?"

I nodded.

"Can't use the fireplace as such. Takes too much of the air." She pointed at the single lamp. "And why we can use only one of these, as well."

A woman came up close to me and smiled. She was young, dark-skinned and held a newborn baby to her breast. I recognized her as the woman in labor on the slave ship.

"Afia, where's Makena? Is he doing better this morning?" Gracie picked up the lamp and walked over to a cot against the wall. I recognized Curly, the man who had been shot by Visitor One. "That's Afia by the way. And this is Makena."

All I could say was, "Pleasure to meet you." What was going on?

To Monsieur St-Amand, Gracie said: "The pigeons are already on board. Makena gave us a good suggestion as to how we could keep them quiet in transit from here to there. Put them in a box inside a sack inside a trunk. But be quick else they smother."

"They're all safe?" he asked.

"All safe."

"Will these two be the only ones going?"

"Three are already on board. And yes. Safe. Two young men and an older woman. Purchased by Muriel yesterday."

"Excellent. How's this man? Fit to travel?" Monsieur St-Amand motioned me over to look at Makena. "What do you think, Dawn?"

I recognized Monsieur St-Amand's work immediately. The wound had been cleaned, sewed up, bandaged, and Makena seemed to be comfortable. "Well done as usual. But when did you ever get time to do this?"

He ignored my question and continued: "What say you carry on with his treatment during the voyage home?"

"Agreed. What are you using against microbes?"

He handed me a bottle. "This."

I took the bottle and tucked it into a pocket in my skirt. "Anything else I should know?"

"You will not be in the cabin we used on the voyage here."

I hadn't thought of this but wasn't surprised.

"You will be in Captain KrommeZee's cabin."

This surprised me and it must have shown on my face.

"He won't touch you."

"Like you didn't want to."

He snapped at me: "Enough!"

A sound behind us made every person in the room turn to look. A woman had entered through the secret panel. Yellow Dress. But today she was wearing a blue dress with her breasts bulging out of the top of it. Her hair was askew and she had colored her cheeks and lips with something to make them rosy and shining.

"You!" said Little Cock, anger welling. "It was you. You tried to steal my hat!"

"The signal worked, didn't it?" She smiled.

Little Cock frowned then relaxed again. "You did that on purpose?"

"I did." With a gentle touch she took his face into her hands. "I recognized Gracie in you. I'm so happy for her. She's known about you for a long time. I'm glad you're safe."

"Thanks only to you, I am."

"What information do you have for us, Muriel?" Gracie. "Good, I pray."

"Very good. We found her and she is on board now as well."

"Excellent. I am so very pleased."

"But they are looking for her."

"Who?" asked Monsieur St-Amand.

Gracie answered: "Violet. The daughter of Silence. Or as she was also known, Tituba."

"You found her daughter?" I slapped my hand over my mouth but I couldn't take back the loudness of my excitement. "Does she know yet?"

"I've sent a messenger to alert James," Yellow Dress said. "He'll get Silence to the ship." To Monsieur St-Amand she said "And I have further good news."

"Yes?"

"We have discovered where her daughter from Samuel Parris is living. Exactly where."

"Excellent."

Yellow Dress put her pointing finger against her lips. "Tell her nothing of this until the plan comes entirely to fruition. Now I have to leave."

"Wait, Muriel. What about the old man and Zuberi the other young boy?"

"They're on their way here. They know they are to wait at the deliveries door. As though seeking work."

Gracie shook her head. "I hate this part. I hate this part."

"What's wrong?" I asked.

Monsieur St-Amand spoke: "Freed slaves are in more danger than those who are owned."

"How can that be? They're free to do as they wish. Go where they wish."

"They aren't," said Gracie. "The men looking for work here in Boston and in other communities hate them. Blame them for stealing the good jobs."

"That's ridiculous."

Monsieur St-Amand said, "It's not easy to understand, especially for someone like you. Someone so…"

"There have been deaths," said Gracie. "Beatings. A free Negro can't get work here without risking his life."

"Why don't they leave then? Hunt? Fish? Start up a farm? A business?"

"No one will give them land. No one will sell to Negroes on credit, either. No work. No money. No food. No shelter. The only ones who'll hire them are the pirates. And the only way to get to the pirates is out at sea. And you need fare to get there."

"Worse than worse, then."

"And even worse than that."

"I'll be off then," said Yellow Dress. "I'll arrange a diversion at the hour of the noon-day meal. The taverns and the other inns will be brimming with men so the streets will have fewer eyes."

"We've not much time, then," said Gracie. "I only hope Silence will be able to make it in time for cast off."

Twenty-six

One by one or two by two as though we had legitimate business in the community, our group slipped out for the docks and Captain KrommeZee's ship. It was soon my turn to leave. I grabbed my munti and another bag and, head bowed, I followed my master, Edward Gooden, through the full dining area out onto the almost empty street.

Yellow Dress was right. Everyone had their midday meal at the same time. Every day. I wondered what this would be like and decided that having such a regimented life, meals always at the same time, always with the same food on the plate and the same beer and wine in the mug or glass, would make for a dull existence. It would leave plenty of time to see to what a neighbor was doing. And disapprove. I much preferred our life near Port Royal. Civilized enough and un-civilized enough. A perfect balance.

As Gracie had predicted, several White men were standing near the old man and the boy called Zuberi at the deliveries door. As we had hoped they would do, the White men chased them away.

"And stay away! Fooking niggers. Honest to Christ, who do they think they are anyway, stealing a God-fearing man's job?" There was much mumbling in agreement. These people were nothing like what I knew among my people. There would be no "each other" here. Ever.

"Yessa, massa. Yessa," the old man called over as he limped along beside me and Little Cock, helped by his much younger companion. He didn't need help, he was lithe and strong, but it was all part of the illusion we were to project.

As we put distance between ourselves and the complaining White men, one of them called out. "And just where do you think you're going? Get back here and shine my shoes." Much laughter.

Then Yellow Dress's voice. Roughened as she acted out to make it sound, I still recognized it. This was her diversion. "Hello, boys. Anyone got a penny or two?"

I glanced back to look. She had her arms around two of the men and was leading them away from the street. A third man reached out to grab the shoulder of one of his companions but when Yellow Dress continued guiding his fellows away, he removed his hand.

Over her shoulder, she called back to him. "For a shilling, I'll do one of you. For two shillings, I'll do one and let another watch. For three shillings…?" Rough laughter.

Not too far ahead of me was a wagon with a big blue trunk in it. Two men pulled it. Even though I saw only their backs, I recognized Woodpecker Food because of his wooden leg, and Bosselé because of his size. They had been part of this plan all along then. Things made sense to me, finally. They walked slowly and carefully and over each bump along the way, they eased it along. Inside the trunk was the injured Makena with Afia's baby. Carrying two heavy bags, Afia walked alongside the wagon. Her step was proud, her head was held high. It was good that she would be leaving for Acadia as soon as she was. She would not survive a master. I didn't think she would even act the part like I was doing. This woman would be of great benefit to our community. Both sides of it.

"Good day, you two," said a male voice from the other side of Little Cock. It was Iggie. Beside him walked a veiled figure.

"Jenny? Is that you in there?"

It was. "They found Violet! They found her! She's on board the ship!"

"Merde," said Iggie.

"What?" Little Cock, Jenny and I asked at the same time.

"Look. It's the *Dowitcher*."

"The what?" I asked.

"The *Dowitcher*. The ship that no doubt has the passengers Benny, Jacques l'Itale and Merit on board. Remember? Its captain refused to sail on a Friday?"

"Merde," I said. "Jenny. Get on the other side of me. Iggie, in front."

We adjusted our positions attempting to hide Jenny among us but we were too late. From the *Dowitcher*, a familiar voice: "*Thar she blows!*" It was Jacques l'Itale, crazier than ever it seemed. He was standing on the rail and holding onto one of the vertical ropes there, his weak condition making the rope shake. His face was gray and mottled. His other hand was waving everywhere as he tried to point at our little knot of people.

We increased the speed of our steps. We were almost there. Almost at the foot of the gangplank. Then we were there. The blue trunk was on board and being set up with ropes to lower it into the hold where it would be safe from prying eyes. Jenny's foot touched the bottom of the gangplank and I pushed her from behind with one hand, my other hand holding my bags. Halfway up the plank, she resisted my push. I looked up. At the top of the gangplank, legs wide, shoulders high, stood Benny, a pistol in each hand. Behind him and to one side, Merit held a musket that pointed toward the sky.

"That's far enough," growled Benny. "You'll not be boarding *this* ship."

From the other ship, Jacques l'Itale's voice: "You can how now, Benjamin. Here we are and there she blows. Nobody knows."

Jacques l'Itale was out of his mind.

Beside me, Little Cock said: "He's not making any sense. What's wrong with him?"

"Brain fever, I'd say."

"He's not looking too good. *Aoup!*"

I was keeping one eye on Benny's two pistols and the other on Merit's musket so didn't see Jacques l'Itale actually fall, but I heard the splash.

Little Cock brushed past me then gently moved the veiled Jenny aside as he passed her to move up the gangplank. From behind his back under his coat he drew out a wide knife as he went. "Looks like your companion has gone for a swim."

"He can take care of himself," said Benny, without inflection in his voice or expression on his face.

Merit's expression changed. He looked down at the spot where Jacques l'Itale had gone under the water. I noticed that several people were jabbing long poles with hooks on them into the garbage that floated between the dock and the *Dowitcher*. "But, sir."

"No buts."

Merit reached an arm around in front of Benny to push his hands with their pistols down. "That's enough, Sir. Our translator is more valuable to us than any runaway slave. And she's back where we were to bring her anyway. Our duty is done." He stepped in front of Benny. "Don't risk yourself now, Sir." To Little Cock he said: "Put that knife away. Let us debark."

Little Cock did not put his knife away. Instead, he held it across his chest with one hand, backed into Jenny and wrapped his other arm across her side. "Touch her? So much as *look* at her and your innards will be leaking into the sea."

The water between the *Dowitcher* and the dock churned. One of the men holding poles called out. "Got 'im hooked but he's shakin' so bad I don't think I can do anything more. Get some more poles over here."

Two more poles descended into the garbage and up came Jacques l'Itale's head and shoulders. He was having a fit so breathing water in. A terrible way to die but at least he would not be aware of it.

Merit ran down the gangplank making it bounce so strongly, it almost sent Benny over into the sea, too.

As Benny passed Little Cock he said. "I will remember you. You can trust me on that."

"That goes both ways."

Over at the other ship, someone had managed to loop a rope around Jacques l'Itale and four men were hauling him up out of the water. Merit stepped in to help. I was experienced with seeing death so I knew that Jacques l'Itale was already gone on his Journey by the time they got him up onto the dock. I felt sorry that he was dead. Not because I would miss him. I wouldn't miss him at all. But I felt sorry that he had contributed so little when he was here.

Captain KrommeZee called out: "All ashore who's going ashore and everybody else get on board. We are leaving before anything else can happen."

I was not sorry about that.

I ran to the ladder leading below decks then down the passageway to the cargo hold two decks down. I opened the first door I came to. Jenny was already there holding her child in her arms. Violet was as beautiful as her mother. Behind Jenny on the floor, the trunk lay open, Makena sat in a chair with many pillows. He appeared to be comfortable and unstressed from being confined in a trunk with a baby. Afia held her tiny child to her breast where it suckled.

We were all safe. Apart from one afternoon of bad weather, the voyage home was without incident. We'd had enough incidents for a lifetime. Or so I chose to believe for the time being. There are many ways to preserve one's sanity and this was mine.

Twenty-seven

Home at last. It seemed that everyone from our village, from Falcon's village, and every soldier from the fort had collected before Captain KrommeZee brought the *Rita Petronella* alongside the dock. Yes. He had finally named his ship. The morning of our arrival at Port Royal, he had hung Lars off the rail to paint her name in bright red paint on both sides of the bow.

When I asked Captain KrommeZee, now Willem to me, why he had taken so long to choose a name, he smiled and said "Couldn't very well name her with that particular name until she had arrived with all her cargo safe, could I? I needed to know that she was worthy of the name."

"Worthy? She isn't named after your wife and your mother-in-law? Pretty names, Rita and Petronella."

"After those two? God—if there is one—forbid!" And he rolled his eyes heavenward anyway making me wonder if he did really believe in a god. "Not even if we were on the bottom at Boston Harbor would I consider it."

He laughed. I didn't.

He explained. "She's named after a man named Peter—not the same Peter who was a friend of Jesus. A more recent man. Peter Claver. There's a great deal of talk about making him the patron saint of slaves and seafarers. How perfect is that for a ship such as this, considering what she was built for? You can name a ship anything you want but I prefer to call it by a woman's name. Hence the feminine form of Peter, Petronella. Petronella's a popular Dutch name. Perhaps having a ship named after him will hurry things along. It takes centuries for those religious buggers to recognize a good man, doesn't it?"

I made no comment. My head was reeling with the coincidences: slaves and seafarers and now a Dutch name for a Dutch captain's ship? If I believed in luck, I knew this would be the luckiest ship that ever sailed.

"They've burned many of those at the stake. Good men, I mean. That's why I have so little use for religious thinking. It starts out as love your neighbor and ends with kill everybody who disagrees with you."

"And the name Rita? Where does that come from?"

"In a way this was in your honor, Keskoua. And in Jenny's honor, too. What a strong woman she is. Look at her. I've hired Pierce, you know."

"Oh. Are you sure—?"

"Don't worry. He'll be away from her for, shall we say, only special voyages? Perhaps twice a year? Most of his work can be done from here in Port Royal. But between him and his niece, and him and Jenny when he's away, and you and Edward Gooden, the air will be so full of message pigeons the sun will be blocked out."

I didn't think that was funny. "Belay that, Willem."

His laugh came right from his toes. "You know that Edward is in love with you, don't you?"

"Belay that, too. I've heard it before. He has a strange way of showing it, doesn't he?"

"He does, but nonetheless, it's true." With his chin, Captain KrommeZee pointed starboard. "There are many kinds of love."

Arms wrapped around Violet, Jenny was sitting on the deck between the two cannons nearest the gangplank. Her face was aglow. Her eyes were half closed. I don't think she had stopped smiling since we left

Boston Harbor. Pierce hovered close by.

"Rita was the patron saint of abused women," Captain KrommeZee said. "Do you approve? Rita Petronella has a nice ring to it. We will know what it means but those who should not know will not."

"It's perfect." I felt water coming into my eyes so turned away from him to search the crowd for my family and there they were.

Nalagit wriggled in Falcon's arms as he turned this way and that looking at everyone. Su'n was the first to see me and jumped up and down waving. When I waved back, Falcon turned Nalagit around and pointed to me. Nalagit saw me, burst into tears then buried his face in Falcon's neck. Taller than he was when I left, Tities dipped his head in a proud bow to me as if he hadn't missed me at all. He ran forward and just as the gangplank kissed the dock, he was on it and up it asking if I needed help to bring anything away.

I pointed to my bag. "This is all I have but first I need a hug from you."

He turned his face away. "Mother."

From the side of my eye I saw several of his friends staring up at us from the dock. "Na t'oq. We can hug later."

"Welaliog, Giju', thanks, Mother." And off he went with my bag.

Claude and Marguerite were there with all nine of their children. Nine? I counted again. Yes. Nine. Plus my daughter, Jeanne. Where did nine—? Ah. The wee thing Claude was holding that looked no more than a bundle of blanket must be the baby Marguerite was carrying before I left. By her smiling, healthy face, I could see that everything was well with her. But I would check on her anyway as soon as I had time to do it.

My brother, Gi'gwesu, had one arm around Wasueg and she had one of her arms wrapped around his waist. It appeared that Wasueg was living up to her name and was blossoming like a flower: from here I would say she was perhaps four months along with what would be my niece or nephew growing inside her. They'd been sharing the cedars for longer than I'd realized. My brother would not be broken hearted after all to learn that Jenny and Pierce had fallen in love with each other. Wasueg would be good for Gi'gwesu and he would take excellent care of her and their child.

***

I learned later, during my time with Marguerite checking her over, that she'd had trouble once again with the birth. This one had come out feet first, too, and the cord was wrapped around the baby's neck. "Rabbit Woman was handling the situation as best she could," Marguerite told me. "But then, out of the blue came Geneviève as though she'd been hiding behind trees for months just waiting to help out. Can you believe that?"

After what I'd been through on my voyage on the *Rita Petronella*, I would believe anything.

A lot had happened while I was away but nothing had changed. The only thing that was different now was the greater fear of New England. And this was not because of Second Son's crazy rantings. Geneviève had sacrificed her own terrors to come back to our village to tell us that the bush was full of English spies. Second Son went around the village now, raising his bottle of rum or whisky or wine in the air and saying "I told you so. I told you so." What was different about this? Second Son was developing a following. Young boys freshly returned from their Spirit Quest. But these boys were already strong, getting their own ideas about how to protect us. Even the Fathers in the local villages were taking up arms and counselling every French person, every Acadian, and even our people to do all in their power to "keep the English heretics out of our land."

"Kill them if you must," Père Bigaud ordered. "We must protect our Catholic faith from those Puritan heathens or those devils will destroy us as a people."

Devils on both sides it seemed. Each side and each underside and overside with its own beliefs and ways of praying, hoping, wishing, desiring. Priests' magic, chenoo magic or witches' magic? Which was the strongest? Which one would save us? No. You have to make your own magic and believe in that and until you do, you are in danger of being swept away with nothing of your own self left.

Acknowledgements

Phyllis Bohonis, Evelyn Crete, Suzanne Keeptwo, Catina Noble, Sue Pictou, Marcel St-Amand, and Joe Wilmot, I can't thank you enough!

About the Author

Sherrill Wark is an editor who designs print/digital books for indie authors. She's the author of: *Really Stupid Writing Mistakes: How to Avoid Them* (non-fiction); *Transplanted Heads: Your Muse Can't Write Worth Sh*t* (blog); *Death in l'Acadie: a Kesk8a story* (historical fiction and the first in a planned 6-book series about life and often violent death in Acadia between 1670–1755 from the 1st Person viewpoint of a Mi'qmaw woman); *Mostly of Love & the Perils Thereof: The Sequel* and *The Closet Hides a Set of Stairs* (poetry). Under her pseudonym Christina Crowe, she has published *A Girl Dog's Breakfast*, scary stories and rude poems and *The Unkindest Cut: Short Creepy Movie Scripts.* Sherrill is also a screenwriter and has finished three screenplays: *The Soul Eaters* (Sci-Fi), *Skin Eater* (serial killer stuff), and *The Bus to Lo Siento* (drama) which landed in the top 10% (out of 600) in the 2013 Oaxaca Film Fest.

On her paternal grandmother's side, she is an Acadian descendant of Claude Guidry and Marguerite Petitpas.

List of Words

amaljugwej: raccoon

apalqaqamej: chipmunk

aplíkmuj: rabbit, hare

apo'qatej: woodpecker; variant spelling(s): apo'qajej (Nova Scotia) , apo'qwatej Alternate forms: apo'qatejg, woodpeckers (plural); apo'qatejl, a woodpecker (fourth person)

app: repeat [please]; what did you say?

apugji'j: mouse; apigji'jg, mice (plural); apigji'jl, apigji'tl, a mouse (fourth person); Nutat apigji'j?; Do you hear the mouse?; Variant spelling(s): apugji'j (Nova Scotia)

atsco, as chu, or wad chu: hill

atu'tuej: squirrel

chenoo: a wendigo

e'e: yes

elue'wiet: crazy

emtesgit: arrogant, snooty

gajuewj: cat

gapjagwej: robin; gapjagwejg: robins; gapjagwejl: a robin

ga'qaquj: crow

gesgamugwa'latl, gesgamugwa'toq: make vanish, make disappear, dissolve

gesmi'sit: speak in odd or unusual way; speak with a heavy accent

gesm'pisit: strange clothes

gi'gwesu: muskrat

gi'gassuinu: teaser, joker

Giju': Mother, Mom

glmuej: mosquito; glmuejg, mosquitoes (plural); glmuejl, a mosquito (fourth person)

gtigiewinuj: drunkard; gtigiewinujg, drunkards (plural); gtigiewinujl, a drunkard (fourth person)

guow: pine; Mesgilg guow gaqamit nignaq, A large pine stands in our yard. Alternate forms: guaq, pines (plural): guowl, a pine (fourth person)

gwitn: canoe; gwitnn, canoes

Haudenosaunee: a Nation ("Iroquois")

jenteg: quiet

kaksk'us, kaksk'ug: cedar(s)

lentug: deer

Lnu Saqamaw: Chief

lutmaqan: gossip, rumor, hearsay

mala'sit: not doing well (health), progressing slowly

masgwi: white birch tree; masgwi'g, white birch trees (plural); masgwi'l, a white birch tree (fourth person)

massa: great

massawachusett: great mountain place

melgwisgat: nightmare; frightened (from nightmare); Miawitpa'qap ngwis melgwisgat aq mu'gisiapajinpagup. It was midnight when my son had a nightmare and then he couldn't go back to sleep. Alternate forms: melgwisgai, I have a nightmare (first person singular animate); melgwisgaieg, We have a nightmare (first person dual exclusive animate); melgwisga'tieg, We have a nightmare (first person plural exclusive animate)

mesgei': I am sorry

mess or mass: great

messatossec: Great hills mouth

Mi'gmaw, Mi'gmaq: Eastern Nation of Aboriginal People

mi'jan: excrement

Mirligueche—present day Lunenburg NS

mi'watm: I am grateful; mi'watmeg: we are grateful

moqopa'q: wine

moqwa': no

mtesgm: snake; mtesgmug, snakes (plural); mtesgml, a snake (fourth person)

mui'n: bear

mulumgwej groundhog, woodchuck

munti: bag, sack

nalagit: energetic, swift, eager

natawinpiteget: good healer

na to'q: all right, OK

nepat: sleep, asleep

oqoti: term of endearment between spouses

sec, sac or saco: mouth

snawe'l, snawe'g: sugar tree(s), maple(s)

su'n: cranberry

tities: bluejay; titiesg: bluejays (plural); titiesl: a bluejay (fourth person)

tmgwalignej; crane, heron; tmgwatinejg, cranes (plural); tmgwatinejl, a crane (fourth person), Enm'papga'timg jijuaqa nemu't tmgwatignej etliwsget gigjiw sitmug, Going down the coast sometimes one can see a heron fishing for food by the shore.

toqosingig: sleep together

toqwa'q: autumn

tqoqwej: lynx

tugwiet: wake up, awaken

tutji'j: little daughter Jugu'wa tutji'j apoqonmatinej, Come little daughter, let us help each other.

wasueg: flower, blossom, bloom, [blossoming flower]

Wendat: a Nation ("Huron")

welaliog: thank you

List of Names

Afia—African slave

Aideen—servant of James Hunter

Apalqaqamej aka Apal—wife of Second Son

Apugji'j—young village woman

Bearded Braid—crew member on slave ship

Benny—slave hunter from New England

Big Meadow—Grand Pré

Bobcat—village Brave

booty fellow—buddy, pal, guy

Bosselé aka Terrence—crew member

Cabin Boy—cabin boy

Captain—Little Cock's pirate ship captain

Charlotte aka Damoiselle Autoritaire—Mathieu's "girlfriend" and cousin of Marguerite

Claude Guidry—friend of Keskoua; husband of Marguerite Petitpas

Aideen—servant of James Hunter

Dupuy—coureur de bois

Falcon—Keskoua's husband

François—Hélène's husband

Geneviève—friend and teacher of Keskoua

Georges—son of François and Hélène

Gi'gwesu—Keskoua's brother

Gilla—Dupuy's woman

Gracie Waite—owner of the Blind Pig Inn
Green Dress—works for/with Yellow Dress/Muriel
Gregor—crew member
Ham Fellow—dock worker
Hélène aka Feather—friend of Keskoua
Honey-Sop (Richard More)—husband of Vaca Imunda
Iggie—soldier at the fort
Jacques l'Itale—slave hunter; translator for Benny
James Hunter—friend of Monsieur St-Amand
J-B—son of Claude with Marguerite
Jeanne—Keskoua's oldest daughter; adopted by Claude and Marguerite
Jenteg—the stranger
John Indian—Jenteg's husband
Key Man—crew member on slave ship
lapointe—a guard
Lars—crew member
Lilac—Little Cock's kidnapped sister
Little Cock—village drunk
Lnu Saqamaw—Chief
Makena aka Curly—African slave
Marguerite Petitpas—Claude's wife
Marie Hunter—daughter of James Hunter
Martha—woman in crowd
Mathieu—Claude's friend
Merit—slave hunter
Monsieur Hermel St-Amand—the surgeon at the fort
Nalagit (Swift)—son of Falcon and Keskoua
One Eye—crew member on slave ship
One-Eyed Joe—village Brave
Père Bigaud—Père Gaëtan's successor

Persistence—young injured boy

Roger—coachman and "valuable friend" of James Hunter

Ruthie—young injured boy's mother

Second Son—second son of Chief

Singing Bear Cub—village Brave

Skinny Man—dock worker

Sleeping Cougar—village Brave; friend of Falcon

Su'n (Cranberry)—daughter of Falcon and Keskoua

the mother of One-Eyed Joe—"ancestor"; healer

Tities (Bluejay)—son of Falcon and Keskoua

Ti-To (P'tit Thomas)—son of François and Hélène

Tommy—crew member

Tugwiet—young village woman

Vaca Imunda (Elinor Butten)—ship passenger

Violet—daughter of Jenny and John Indian

Visitor One aka Joseph—slave buyer

Visitor Three—slave buyer

Visitor Two—slave buyer

Wasueg (Blossoming Flower)—young village woman

Willem KrommeZee—ship's captain

Woodpecker Food—crew member

Yellow Dress aka Muriel—slave buyer

~~Young~~ Rabbit Woman

Zuberi—young African slave